By the same author
THE COLOUR OF RAIN
THE CRACK
HOTEL DE DREAM
THE BAD SISTER
WILD NIGHTS
ALICE FELL
QUEEN OF STONES
WOMAN BEWARE WOMAN
BLACK MARINA
THE ADVENTURES OF ROBINA

In the 'Cycle of the Sun' series:
THE HOUSE OF HOSPITALITIES
A WEDDING OF COUSINS

For children:
THE SEARCH FOR TREASURE ISLAND
THE GHOST CHILD

◆ *The* ◆
MAGIC DRUM
AN EXCURSION
◆

Emma Tennant

VIKING

VIKING

Published by the Penguin Group
27 Wrights Lane, London w8 5tz, England
Viking Penguin Inc., 40 West 23rd Street, New York, New York 10010, USA
Penguin Books Australia Ltd, Ringwood, Victoria, Australia
Penguin Books Canada Ltd, 2801 John Street, Markham, Ontario, Canada l3r 1b4
Penguin Books (NZ) Ltd, 182–190 Wairau Road, Auckland 10, New Zealand

Penguin Books Ltd, Registered Offices: Harmondsworth, Middlesex, England

First published 1989

10 9 8 7 6 5 4 3 2 1

Copyright © Emma Tennant, 1989

Printed in Great Britain by
Richard Clay Ltd, Bungay, Suffolk
Filmset in Monophoto Plantin

A CIP catalogue record for this book is available from the British Library
ISBN 0-670-825565

Castaly A fountain of Parnassus sacred to the Muses. Its waters had the power of inspiring with the gift of poetry those who drank of them.

Brewer's Dictionary of Phrase and Fable

An exile, I have drunk from the Castalian spring,
But not such water as there rose

Kathleen Raine, 'The Well'

For Tony Lacey

◆ ACKNOWLEDGEMENTS ◆

For permission to reproduce copyright material, grateful acknowledgement is made to the following: Weidenfeld & Nicolson Ltd for the excerpt from *The Savage God* by A. Alvarez; the Peters, Fraser & Dunlop Group Ltd for the excerpt from *The Act of Creation* by Arthur Koestler, published by the Hutchinson Publishing Group Ltd; and Kathleen Raine for the excerpt from 'The Well'.

◆ CONTENTS ◆

◆ PROLOGUE ◆

Cressley Grange (borders of England and Wales; Ludlow 12 miles, Hereford 38 miles) was built in the sixteenth century on the foundations of a Cistercian monastery. Of the monastery the refectory remains, and an arch to the west of the house. In the early eighteenth century a stone façade was imposed on the Elizabethan brick of the south front, giving the impression, from the drive, of a house of much later date and origins. Three sides of Cressley are overhung with creepers, and this emphasizes the contrast with the façade, which is bare and plain. A stone fountain in the shape of a maiden, said to represent the nymph Castalia and recently installed in the forecourt, adds an unexpected note of gaiety. Some visitors liken the house to a work of the imagination, saying the untidy jumble of rooms and staircases, and the confusion of centuries in the old brick house, are the muddle of the unconscious, while the stone façade, with its classical symmetry, is the superimposed formal order essential in a work of art. Visitors to Cressley are, however, encouraged to think like this.

In the 1920s the house was bought by Frederick Cole, a Hereford solicitor. His son, Jason Cole, came into the inheritance – of house and grounds but very little money – in 1955 when he was still at Oxford. Jason Cole received the Kenyon Award for Poetry, and the Somers Prize. After two years as literary editor of the *Listener*, he married the poet Muriel Phrantzes and went to live permanently at Cressley.

Since the tragic death of Muriel Phrantzes Cole in 1967 Cressley Grange has been run as an institute of creative writing by Jason Cole and his cousin Jane Cole. There are never more than six students at a course, and each course lasts five days – from the Friday evening, when the car, driven by Mr Rees, returns from meeting the 18.48 at Hereford, to the following Wednesday at noon. It is always assumed that guests at Cressley have come from and are going back to London; other arrangements, if they are necessary, have to be made tactfully. Jane Cole very much dislikes any alterations to her timetable.

Jason Cole, who lectures and gives readings of his poetry up and down the British Isles, presides at only half a dozen courses at Cressley in a year. As a result, the running of the place is left almost entirely in the hands of Jane Cole. Mrs Rees, who lives with her husband in the lodge cottage, cleans in the house and helps with the cooking. At each writing course (except for those attended by Jason Cole) a professional author is invited to Cressley, to give the 'creative spark' to the students. The fee for this service is £185, rail fare and board included.

Anyone coming unknowingly on Cressley Grange (the gardens are open to the public on Saturdays) would wonder for what crime the occupants of the Grange had been locked up. Behind the tall windows of the eighteenth-century façade, and behind the mullioned windows of the old Elizabethan house, and behind oak doors that lead to the Cistercian refectory, men and women, some no longer young, can be seen scribbling in a notebook or staring at a sheet of paper which, although it is blank, appears to contain their sentence. Even in the old barn in the courtyard at the back of the house, figures can be glimpsed in this same attitude of agonized confinement. It would surprise the casual visitor to the romantic gardens of Cressley Grange to hear that these sufferers are paying for the privilege.

Most of the visitors aren't casual, though. Muriel Cole's reputation has grown to a point where pilgrims to Cressley journey from as far away as the United States or Japan in the hope of spending a few hours in the grounds of the house where their heroine lived and died. Those who try to push their way further – in through one of the innumerable back doors, or into the old barn which was converted in Muriel Cole's day into a two-bedroom annexe – are firmly repelled by Mr or Mrs Rees or by Jane Cole herself. The trespassers are invariably women, usually in their early thirties. All the visitors to Cressley, or nearly all, could be said to fall into this category: the difference between them being that those who try to invade the privacy of the Coles are likely to be American or Canadian, while the English are respectful of property and the literary tradition embodied by Cressley Grange. Greek visitors (Muriel Cole's father was from Salonika) prefer picnicking in the grounds.

In the gloom of a Friday evening in December an estate wagon can be seen going up the drive of Cressley Grange. Amongst the 'students' in the rear seat is Catherine Treger, a journalist on the *Clarion*. She has been assigned to write a piece on (a) can creativity be bought and taught and should government money subsidize it, and (b) the continuing cult of Muriel Cole. It is hoped that the stay at Cressley will yield new insights into the creative process and the vexed question of the taxpayer, while the much-mined subject of Muriel Cole may on this occasion yield something fresh. For a previously unknown novel by the poet has recently been discovered at Cressley. (Various extracts have been published recently, and one

xiii

appeared last week in the *Guardian*, which has caused some annoyance to *Clarion* features editor John Carpenter and has compelled him to commission this article in which Catherine Treger is expected to 'dig up' new facets of the personality and life of Muriel Cole.) Rumour has it that the sum of $1.2 million has been paid in the US for the rights to the novel – payment going to Jason and Jane Cole, trustees of the estate.

The car stops in front of the house. Lights go on in the hall, and the front door opens. Jane Cole stands there, right arm outstretched in welcome. It would be no surprise to hear a bunch of keys jangle at her waist, as one by one she greets the voluntary prisoners and lets them in.

Catherine Treger's
DIARY

◆

◆ FRIDAY ◆

8.30 p.m.

Am still trying to find my way round Cressley Grange. Coming up from supper (if you can call it that) I took a left on the first landing – which I'm sure I was told to do when we were shown our rooms earlier – and came slap up against a cupboard! It's like a house in an old-fashioned murder story – you almost expect Agatha Christie to appear from the faded chintzes and hand you a green Penguin of *The Murder of Roger Ackroyd*. At the same time, I can see why the house had such a haunting quality for Muriel Cole. There's something secret about the winding passages, and the recesses, and the rooms with different height ceilings that make you feel you've gone from a church to a burrow, and from one century to another, like moving in a dream. All of Muriel Cole's best poems were written here (it was interesting to see her portrait in the sitting-room: although it's been reproduced a million times, her face looks much stronger in the original).

I think I may have quite a good time here, though to begin with I didn't want to leave London, and Richard didn't want me to go, and even John Carpenter looked as if he knew he was scraping the barrel with this particular idea. Like all features editors, John dreads the Christmas season. The 'think' pieces that stultify the bored and surfeited readers even further, and the obligatory short story he never wanted to commission, and the recipes for time-saving entertaining, all put him in a mood that is alternately irascible and sulky. 'Stress the money side when you've dug up something new on Muriel Cole,' he said as I was zipping up my typewriter to go. 'The big advance for the new novel. Try and get an extract, by the way. And show the absurdity of a bunch of nuts going to a country house in the expectation of catching a dose of creativity – and the government actually subsidizing it!'

'It's a long piece,' I said. 'And as I'm sure there's nothing new on Muriel Cole, I'll have to put in a lot of atmosphere, like ghosts and snowstorms, just to fill it out.'

'I'll put it on the Women's Page,' he threatened after me.

Richard wasn't much better when I said I was being sent to the borders of Wales at a time when his family invariably comes over from Australia for the festive season. He looked at me suspiciously – he was in the middle of pulling off a polo-neck jumper and as his eyes were pulled upwards they seemed to bulge with accusation – and he said, 'I suppose you think you can run away from it this year. You know it's their first weekend. You know they're expecting –'

'Five hot meals,' I said.

'Suppose you get snowed up?' Richard said.

'Well, what if I do?'

'If we have a small child, you'll hardly be able to rush off like this just before Christmas,' Richard said.

'But we haven't got a small child,' I said.

When Richard gets like this I feel I can't stay with him a day longer. Maybe the family visit gives him claustrophobia – think of having Melanie as your sister, not to

The Little Bookshop

1 Cheapside, Ambleside, Cumbria LA22 0AE
Telephone: (015394) 32094

The Magic Dra

w f(o pnt

mention the parents – but I feel I'm meant to be the real mother, providing all the meals etc., and defending him from his own relatives at the same time. If I didn't come back for Christmas, what would Richard do? But that's idle conjecture. I've got to finish this piece and get it in to John Carpenter or I'll have lost a job as well as gaining Richard's family. In the New Year, though, when they've gone back . . .

Jane Cole just stuck her head round the door. 'We're going to meet downstairs for coffee and readings in thirty minutes,' she said. Now she's gone down the landing, telling the others. Apparently, the way the 'students' get to know each other on the first night is by reading their latest efforts aloud to each other. I can't think of anything more pulverizing! Thank God I haven't got to read out my latest article in the *Clarion*!

A few first impressions before it's time to go down.

The drive to Cressley was pretty boring because it was dark, but I had this odd feeling in the bus that some of the 'students', or maybe all of them, were suffering from first-degree nerves. There was a high-tension, snappy atmosphere – the young man I sat next to, who said his name was Joe Merton, nearly bit my head off when I asked him what his ambitions in life were. (Is it a very tactless question? Did I mind it when I was his age? Probably.) He said he certainly wasn't going to be a journalist. I was clearly meant to feel snubbed. He was a poet, he said. I pointed out it was hard to live on poetry. To rile him? He gave me a funny look, which I more sensed than saw in the dark! 'Do or die,' he said. He sounds as if he's going to be rather an old-fashioned poet!

The other feeling of slight tension I picked up – *frisson* is too strong a word – was when a woman (dark, late

5

forties, and wedged up against Mr Rees the driver) asked Mr Rees how long he had been driving this particular car. She has a strong foreign accent. Mr Rees seems to have known her in the past, because they were joking together. (I wonder what she's doing on the course. Improving her English?)

'The car was new last week,' Mr Rees said. He sounded proud of it. 'Ford. Estate Wagon.' The foreign woman – she introduced herself later as Gertrud Ritchie, and that was her husband on the other side – gave a loud laugh. 'Literary estate wagon,' she said. 'Or shall we say, band wagon?'

This was all rather odd, as some of the 'students' must have felt, because they gave uneasy titters, like school-children found laughing at the headmaster. Perhaps Gertrud Ritchie will be able to tell me some Cole family secrets for the piece.

Supper was tiny portions of cottage pie and Heinz tomato soup first. I already feel hungry. Wish I'd at least brought some biscuits.

I don't think I'll get much from Jane Cole. After our first welcome on the doorstep, she showed just how distant she intended to be. We were taken into the refectory – a splendid old room with stone arches and a great oak table running down the middle, and then she led us through into a sitting-room where a fire – thank goodness – was burning. One of the youngest 'students', a girl of about nineteen with mousy hair tied back and rather staring, pale blue eyes, gasped and cried out when she saw the picture over the massive stone fireplace was a portrait of Muriel Cole. And it *is* an arresting picture. The most Greek aspect of the poet is brought out in it: black eyes, high cheekbones, a golden colour to the skin which was probably sallow in real life, but in the softly lit room at

6

Cressley is like pure, Greek gold. Jane Cole moved (protectively?) in front of the fireplace at the sound, and fixed the unfortunate girl with an unnerving stare.

'You like the painting of Muriel?'

The girl nodded. She looked as if the whole thing was too much for her: arrival at Cressley, with its dark passages, and stone halls hung with tapestries, and the knowledge that she was under the roof that had sheltered Muriel Cole – and then had perhaps not sheltered her enough, for why otherwise would she have decided to leave for another world?

'We don't discuss the work of Muriel Cole on these courses,' Jane Cole said. 'We talk about the potential of the students. About Promise.' She glanced round the room – I could almost hear the keys jangle. The others carefully avoided looking at the poor girl, as if she were already being punished for worshipping at the wrong shrine and they were disowning heresy. Jane Cole finished with the announcement that we would all meet in an hour, and that Jason Cole is expected to arrive tomorrow. There was a slight ripple of excitement at the news, although everyone must have known he would be on the course – they wouldn't have booked it otherwise. Maybe it's just his name, and his good looks, and the tragic past – Jason Cole is a legend in his lifetime, though he wouldn't be without Muriel Cole, I suppose. Gertrud, the woman who made the sour remarks in the car, went quite red at the sound of his name. Is something going on there, perhaps? I'll have to get all the names right later, to interview them in the duration of the course on what they're getting out of it.

Asked Jane Cole for an interview tomorrow. Rather icily, she gave me 12.30 p.m.

MURIEL COLE:
Biog. notes for article

Muriel Phrantzes Cole (1935–1967). Greek father, English mother (they divorced in 1948). Brought up mainly England, attended St Paul's Girls' School. (See *Letters to the man who was once my father*.) Lady Margaret Hall, Oxford (1954); left before her finals to marry Jason Cole (see *Apotheosis*, first volume of collected poems, 1956). The second collection, *Chimaerae* (1958) won high esteem. It was followed by *Stultifera Navis* in 1960, the year in which she was awarded the Ellenberg Memorial Prize. *Shells*, her last volume, was published posthumously in 1968.

Since then, more has been written and spoken about Muriel Cole than about any other artist born within the last half-century. She is seminal to the feminist movement in America – and more so than Sylvia Plath, whose work made a good deal of impact at first, but was passed over in favour of Muriel Cole on the grounds that the latter was better able to give expression to women's profounder feelings of rage, guilt and neglect.

◆

Do I sound bitchy here? I think it's difficult for me to know what my feeling for Muriel Cole's poetry really is. Like most women, I identified immediately with the pain and sense of loss (why, I wonder? If only we knew). But after a while I found it did me more good *not* to read it. Some feminists say I'm keen on improving my own position and am an enemy of the movement. Maybe I am, but they seem priggish and self-righteous to me. Using Muriel Cole's misery to bolster their own sense of inadequacy, they never stop whining – well, I'd better not get carried away again. I've every respect for those women who work

8

for equal opportunities, equal pay, etc. But I can't help feeling Muriel Cole has done more harm than good, not that she could have guessed what was coming, of course.

Since her death, critics have been busy re-defining Muriel Cole's reputation. It's an enormous industry. Sales of Muriel Cole books must be gigantic – and now the undiscovered novel is going for $1.2 million! Also, there seems to be an unending stream of poems and fragments of poems – once suppressed by Muriel, I suppose, as not measuring up to her high standards, but invaluable material now, as the Coles slowly release them, for judging the entire canon of work up until her death. They must bring in quite a whack from American universities and the like, although the novel must be the longest and most important work to surface for some time. How galling for Muriel Cole, who never made a penny from her work, and deeply resented her financial dependence on the Cole family, to support them now in luxury! But all this is going on as if she were still alive, which shows how powerful the legend of her has become.

As for the suicide, I just can't go along with the view that creative women, once confronted with domesticity, have no option other than self-immolation. I know Virginia Woolf started all this, with her remark that the soul of an artist born into a woman's body is a disastrous combination, but it's gone too far these days. (Or do I feel this because, at thirty-three, I've never married or had a child?) No – Muriel Cole gave herself an overdose of morphine because she had been in actual physical pain for some years – a fact her supporters, with their emphasis on the psychological, conveniently gloss over. The car accident in which she broke her leg and also miscarried her child (see 'Applecart' in *Shells*) was three years before she ended her life. She often had to take heavy doses of

9

painkillers. The morphine she procured in the end was no stranger to her (see 'After Sister Morphine', ibid.). And if every woman with an unfaithful husband took to the syringe with such promptitude, the human race would quickly die out.

Jane Cole banged on my door and came in. Found myself covering this up, as if the subject of the death of Muriel Cole weren't permissible. I suppose it isn't, here.

'Time to come down,' she said. I wondered for a moment if she was going to call me Miss Treger. In the end, she didn't call me anything.

'Great,' I said. I felt ill at ease: Jane Cole, though putting on a pleasant face, seemed in some way hostile to me.

'This is Muriel's old room, you know,' Jane Cole said.

Then she went down the stairs. Suddenly – ridiculously – feel rather spooked. Might ring Richard after the readings and see what's happening at home.

11.30 p.m.

Good God! What a performance! I'm glad, like any travelling hack journalist, that I brought a bottle of Scotch in my suitcase. Would like to lie down and flake out, but must write up these notes now, as tomorrow will be a busy day.

We all collected in the sitting-room – this time I remembered how to get there. The main trouble with the layout at Cressley is that there are too many staircases. A tiny, oak staircase leads up from the refectory to Jason Cole's private apartments (Jane Cole shouted at the young girl with staring eyes who tried to go up it after supper: the girl went scarlet with embarrassment). The wide staircase that led me by mistake into a cupboard is similar in appearance – cord-carpeted, high banisters – to the one that takes me up to the landing where my room is, but it's at the other end of the small hall between the refectory and the sitting-room, and somehow they both look like reflections of stairs in a mirror. I haven't discovered where the 'wrong' one goes yet, but the two young men came down opposite me as I was going down, and one of them muttered about not having been in a dormitory since leaving school. Maybe those are the bachelors' quarters!

Have come more and more to the conclusion that people who go on courses like this fall into stereotypes. Don't know how far I can go with this for the *Clarion*, but readers might enjoy feeling they can visualize these 'nutters', as John Carpenter so kindly calls them. (And as our Education Supplement editor would be furious to hear them called.)

STEREOTYPES

Joe Merton Early twenties. The ambitious young man who snubbed me in the car, and who clearly dislikes being in a dormitory. Typical example of a middle-class graduate, family probably from Surrey, with a faked 'regional' accent. He read his poems, which at least are fairly short. I'm not competent to judge, but they made no sense to me. There was a lot of blood and hatred in them. He hardly deigned to read them to us because he's waiting for one thing only – he's been waiting, he said, since he started writing poetry at the age of twelve – and that's the opinion and advice of Jason Cole. Slight brown moustache. Square head. Not as tall when he stands up as you think he's going to be.

Lana Traill The girl who can't take her eyes off the portrait of Muriel Cole. She may be a little older than nineteen, but she has a retarded childlike personality. Hair tied back with a piece of string. Said she did automatic writing. Read some of it. I'd rather listen to an automatic dishwasher. Then she read a short lyric, very Muriel Cole-influenced. Jane Cole smiled at her quite kindly when she had finished.

Pamela Wright When we all got off the 18.48 at Hereford, I was surprised to see this woman with iron-grey hair in a bun, bulky donkey jacket etc., come forward in response to Mr Rees's inquiry. Now I see she fits in perfectly as a stereotype. She's a widow, lives in a village near Birmingham, and she's brought the young boy with her – the one who was coming down the stairs with Joe Merton. Particularly interested in deprived kids. Hopes to be inspired by Jason Cole's new methods of getting poetry through to those with literacy problems. A *Guardian* reader, not a *Clarion* reader. Has a slight limp, complained of the damp affecting her sciatica.

Ken Pamela Wright's protégé: she probably met him through a Birmingham country holiday scheme. Just left the comprehensive and working in a factory. Punk hair, punk mirror specs, and a cross little mouth, which is almost swallowed up by a dirty grey polo-neck. Pamela Wright clearly thinks he's Rimbaud and he may well be of the same opinion. Refused to read. Completely silent all evening. Almost certainly on drugs.

Paul and Gertrud Ritchie Late forties or older. First sight, they seem to have been married quite a time, then one begins to wonder. Their fed-up-ness with the

world and each other could equally be the first disillusion-
ment or the last throes. Paul is a lecturer in English at
Exeter University, and from the way he referred to his
'stuff' he's a failed poet as well. Spoke quite a lot about
'Jason' – they must be old friends from Oxford, with Jason
shooting ahead and leaving the other with the Glittering
Prize of one volume of coolly greeted poems. He read one
of them, which was of the 'I saw you walk down the street /
Then you were gone' variety, and Jane Cole made en-
couraging noises of a particularly damning kind. Short,
stocky, good-looking but features too small and neat.

Gertrud Ritchie seems more interesting. She's doing a
thesis on Jason Cole's poetry for Berlin University – has
obviously known him for some time too, but not for as
long as Paul, and has come down here to ask some questions. Not very attractive, but could be to men, I suppose:
black hair with a straight fringe, a pointed chin, and an
affected old-fashioned flirtatious way of behaving (tossing
hair, sing-song voice, head to one side), which would suit
a don's wife of the Fifties better than now. I was wrong, I
think, in imagining there had been some romantic liaison
with Jason Cole: the truth is more surprising. After a
glass or two of the mulled wine which Jane Cole ladled
out when the reading was over, Gertrud came up and
tossed her hair etc., preparatory to speaking (by the time
they're getting older, women like that forget how to talk
to women).

'You're Catherine Treger? From the *Clarion*, Jane
said?'

'Yes.'

'Do you – do you know my husband Paul Ritchie's
poetry at all?'

'No. No, I'm afraid I don't.'

'Oh. You're doing a piece I suppose on . . .'

13

She floundered for a word. Despite the German accent, she speaks so fast it's hard to believe she could ever become inarticulate. I felt like suggesting *Zeitgeist* as the word she was looking for.

'On what happens here when creative people are gathered together,' Gertrud said. 'I think you should interview Paul, you know. He has so much experience. And he is an old friend of Jason's.'

'Of Muriel's too?' I said.

I would say here that Gertrud Ritchie stiffened, except that any self-respecting creative writing school would throw it out as a cliché.

'Of course, he knew her.' Then she thought of another way of getting publicity for her husband. She lowered her voice. 'Paul can tell you *all* about Muriel,' she said.

That wasn't the interesting part, though. Journalists without number have met drunken poets who 'would tell everything that happened in the life of Muriel Cole – see you at the French pub', or, 'Why-don't-you-give-me-lunch-at-the-Caprice-and-I'll-tell-you' – and then got nothing that wasn't already in the biographies, memoirs or the poet's own letters to Greece. But Gertrud Ritchie had something to add. She leaned forward, until her 'curtain of hair' was swinging right in my face.

'I have told you that I am writing a thesis on Jason Cole's poems of 1955 to 1975? Well, "The Revellers", the most important poem in the years 1963 and 1964 –'

Here, Gertrud broke off. Jane Cole was bearing down on us at full steam, with a silver tray covered in wine glasses held in two hands and a large handbag rocking on a strap from her left arm. She looks like an Indian chief: high cheekbones, lanky black hair parted down the middle, and a caftan that could have served as a wigwam to a whole tribe.

14

'Gertrud, I'd like you to help a little, if you don't mind. Over there . . .' She waved the tray in the direction of the fireplace. The glasses slid about, while the handbag swayed violently. 'I think Paul's having a little trouble,' she went on. 'So . . .'

Gertrud turned back to me when Jane Cole had moved off in the direction of the door into the hall. One glance at the fireplace showed that Joe Merton, who was red in the face, was attacking the older poet and lecturer at Exeter University. Paul Ritchie stood with his back to the fire with a tired, pained expression on his face – but seemed rather pleased, too, I thought, in the absence of Jason Cole to be taken seriously enough as a poet to be attacked. Merton was raising and shaking his fist like a Punchinello that jumps out of a box.

'Muriel *sacrificed* herself for "The Revellers",' Gertrud said. 'You realize I'm telling you this because when my investigations are completed after leaving here, I shall make my discovery known. I count on you, of course, not to ring it straight through to your editor this evening, but I think I can rightly say that you now have a scoop.'

'The Revellers'? Even I know that this long, lyric poem is considered the crowning achievement of Jason Cole's career. Critics have complained that nothing since has come near to it in sheer beauty and intensity. At the same time, I thought Gertrud Ritchie must be drunker than she appeared. And the row over by the fire was getting worse, with Joe Merton shouting, 'bloody snobbish little minimalist', or that's what it sounded like – and poor little Lana Traill standing under the portrait of Muriel Cole with an almost frightening look of adoration on her face.

'Muriel did everything for Jason,' Gertrud said. 'And after "The Revellers" was finished, she died. He was writing *her* death sentence in it, you know. Wasn't it terrible?'

15

This time there was a distinct slur in Gertrud's voice. She began to walk rather slowly and uncertainly in the direction of her husband – from the back, in her flowered dress, she looked like an armchair that was being wheeled across the room. I went after her.

'How do you know?' I said.

Gertrud looked straight into my face this time, without shaking her hair or laying her head on one side. She gave an unexpected answer. 'Computer word-analysis.' She smiled when she saw the expression on my face. 'Didn't you see the piece on Sholokov's *And Quiet Flows the Don*?'

I had to admit I hadn't. And Gertrud didn't have time to explain how a computer can detect the hidden meanings of the writer, because Paul Ritchie marched over from the fireplace and took her arm firmly. 'I've had enough of this,' he hissed. 'Time for bed,' he said more loudly. Before Jane Cole, who had just reappeared from the kitchen, could stop him, he guided Gertrud out of the room and up the stairs.

Well, it's certainly something to be told that one of England's most famous living poets was not above concealing cryptic messages in his best work. If Gertrud Ritchie is telling the truth, of course. John Carpenter may cheer up when he hears this. Is Gertrud going to confront Jason Cole with her new knowledge this weekend? What will he do?

After the Ritchies went up to bed, Jane Cole decided to end the evening. It transpires that Pamela Wright is in the room next to mine, and as Jane Cole went round putting out the lights, we agreed about use of bathroom etc. (the bathroom is opposite). The young Rimbaud, Ken, went up the opposite stairs after Joe Merton. No one made any mention of Joe Merton's behaviour, so I

16

suppose it's quite common amongst poets and would-be poets to get into fights.

Jane Cole went up the same stairs as Joe and Ken and called down good-night as she went. I was a bit surprised by this. Hadn't she noticed that she hadn't turned off the picture-light above Muriel's portrait, and that Lana Traill was still standing under it? I suggested to Pamela Wright that she go into the bathroom first – although we'd just agreed on the other way round – and went back into the sitting-room. It seemed irreligious to break the silence, but surely the poor girl ought to be told to go to bed?

'Lana,' I said.

Lana Traill swung round so sharply that I jumped. She gave me a sort of blank look, like sleepwalkers are meant to have, and then swung back, this time much more slowly, to resume her stance under the picture.

I must confess that, with all the other lights off in the room, Muriel did look like some beautiful icon, the flat, gold face and black eyes looking out in peace and sorrow at the darkened room. (It's odd, but whenever people write of Muriel, the writing always goes all sloppy. I'm obviously no exception – it's just my first time at it.)

'Isn't she fantastic?' Lana said quietly.

'Yes. But you ought to go to bed, Lana. I mean, if you want to work tomorrow.'

Lana turned again, and this time the blank look had completely gone. Hatred shone in her eyes. 'I'm not working with him,' she said. She clenched her fist and held it against her chest, as if in self-defence.

'Working with whom?'

'With Jason Cole. He should have been the one to go. I'm not working with Muriel Cole's husband.'

Oh dear, oh dear. I expect the Coles get quite a few

fanatics of this description – they can't really vet everyone who comes on a course, and no doubt the girl was recommended by a college somewhere. Should I tell Jane Cole about her? Better work that out in the morning when I have my interview.

It wasn't difficult in the end getting Lana to bed, except it turns out she's sleeping in the converted barn and we had to unbolt an ancient back door to let her out. There was a new moon, and frost, and I would have felt cold and rather uneasy if I'd been Lana, having to walk over the courtyard and into the shadows of the barn. But she said she wasn't on her own there. It seems the Ritchies are next door, thank goodness. (With people like Lana Traill, you start worrying at once. I suppose they want you to.)

How would I describe Muriel's room for *Clarion* readers? Well, it's fairly large, about four metres long and impossible to say how wide because of all the uneven bits – the recesses, and what seems to be a bricked-in fireplace, and a round alcove, like a turret, with a dressing-table and a chair in it. It's odd to think of Muriel sitting there, brushing her hair. Jet black hair. She was like one of the unlucky princesses in a fairy story, the black-haired one, who has a red rose tree grow- ing outside her window instead of the white roses of the favoured golden-haired sister. Did everything go wrong for her because she willed it to, in some perverse way? Her poems, prescriptions for suicide – did she write them without knowing what she was doing and then let them send her to her death?

(Keep all above for article if no hard facts.) I must go to bed. I wish there had been some answer when I tried to call Richard, though.

A strange thing: just now, as I went round the room

18

putting out lights, I saw a door I didn't notice before. The far side of the room by the bed. I thought this room was at the end of the corridor. But my room – Muriel's room – must adjoin another. I'll never get Cressley right! But I look forward to seeing the grounds in the morning.

◆ SATURDAY ◆

8.30 a.m.

Before going down to breakfast, must record the rather embarrassing thing that happened last night, or, I suppose in the early hours of this morning.

I didn't sleep well. Never have, in a strange bed. And the one here couldn't be stranger. It's a four-poster, and very high, so I felt like the Princess and the Pea – more princesses again, that must be the influence of Muriel. When I did sleep, I kept having the same dream over and over again: the bed I was in was a boathouse, built out over water, and I was lying asleep in it. Then I opened my eyes at a very light brush on the cheek. A woman with long, black hair was staring intently at me. Then she flitted away. And I woke properly. I'm not superstitious, but when the dream went on repeating itself I felt quite horrible, like a child trying to fight fear in the night.

What really *did* wake me from one of the repeat showings of the dream was a loud crash that seemed to come from the back of the bed. I sat up – more sounds, from behind the wall, I realized – the wall that the bed was pushed up against – the wall with the unexpected door in it. I know I shouldn't have done this, but I crept out of bed and went to try the handle of the door. My heart was thumping in the most ridiculous way. If someone had broken into Cressley Grange, or if Lana Traill had somehow made her way into the house and was freaking out

20

somewhere, I'd better report to authority. Although the thought of trying to find Jane Cole's room in this labyrinth, and then of waking that inscrutable, hostile Red Indian face, wasn't something I fancied overmuch.

The door was a bit stiff, but in the end it opened a crack, and I stared through.

The man standing in the next room was tall, and stark naked. There was quite a bright light on, and the room looked as if it had been rushed into, rather than entered – there was a rucksack, half-open and spilling out shirts on to the floor. A mass of papers on the desk. There were some African and pre-Columbian masks on the wall, and a drum by the side of the bed.

A naked body is still so unacceptable a figure in our society (I'll have to leave the *Clarion* and join *New Statesman and Society* if I start writing like this) that it took what seemed to be ages for my mind to reject it, digest it and then to recognize that it belonged to Jason Cole. Everyone knows his face, it's on the covers of his books, it's on posters at all poetry festivals, it's always in the papers etc. It's a thin, powerful face, with dark, heavy-lidded eyes, more American Indian than Jane Cole, if possible – it must run very strongly in the family for cousins to look so alike.

The worst is that he saw me. Or he sensed my eye, and then saw it.

I was petrified. I closed the door and stood behind it. But nothing happened. Except he laughed loudly, as I crept along the skirting of the wall like a mouse, on my way back to bed.

I went off to sleep finally, feeling I was the one who had appeared ridiculous.

10.30 a.m.

What a beautiful place Cressley is!

Everything is perfect. The lawns are so green and smooth (gardeners paid for by the Muriel Cole Trust, as I ascertained from Mrs Rees just now in the kitchen), the Welsh mountains give just the right blueness and distance, and it's a fantastic morning as well. Cressley is in a narrow valley, its own cul-de-sac, and the house is up at the far end, so you get the secure, strange feeling of being in a place where no one could come up and surprise you from the back, while in front you can survey the country for miles around.

Various paths lead out of this haven, winding away from the gardens and the sycamore drive and into woodland, most of which is bare now, of course, but there are some splendid old yews, and holly berries fatter and redder than any I've seen. All in all, I can understand why Muriel felt so drawn to the place. The only part I don't feel is right here is the severe eighteenth-century façade: the red-brick house fits in so perfectly with the slope of the ground, and the winding paths and shrubberies, that grey stone, and pediments like disapproving eyebrows, do seem to interject a note almost of reproof. Never mind – it's fun to think that the front of the house is like a mask, and you could peel it off any time, to find the real house underneath.

The other thing about Cressley is that every tree and bush looks as if it had been planted in just the right place – as if some magical master-plan was consulted every time new planting was needed. Maybe that's why one has that

22

uncanny feeling of recognition, of having been here before: that there is in fact a symbolic meaning to the positioning of the flowers and plants, and the landscape as a whole 'means' something. But I'm probably getting too fanciful here. Muriel's Cressley poems must have left their mark – 'Ash Tree', for instance, or 'Excavating the Barrow'. I saw the Ash Tree as soon as I looked out of my window this morning. It's right under the window, Muriel's window. 'Now the ash weeps in a hoop of iron/And I dance alone inside./Old witch, witch-hazel, pussy-willow bride.'

And when I took one of the paths to the right, leading up from the garden on the south side of the woodland, I came almost immediately on the famous barrow. At first it was difficult to tell it from the simulated mounds the eighteenth century loved to put in its gardens. There are plenty of those, another factor in making one feel pleasantly at home, for the little inclines and drops are like the interior of the old house, where most of the rooms have two or three steps leading up to them. The woodland garden is, in winter, like the skeleton of a house. The trees are a rough framework of beams, enclosing rooms in barrows and mounds.

Some of these thoughts must have come in remembering Muriel's poem. I'd always had such a strong picture of the sturdy little wood that followed a stream down into the valley of Cressley – and the barrow inside the wood, where – as in a Muriel Cole poem – 'a man lay frozen dead for a millennium' and his leather and iron too. But it took some time to find the barrow. The raw wound Muriel saw when the men slashed open the top of the tomb had been healed with gorse and bracken. Only the steep sides of the mound give the show away – they're impossible to climb, and their sheerness makes you realize suddenly that you're

23

standing right by a burial place. Not that they found the bones of a man there, of course. Just a few shards, broken pots and the like.

I knew I had to get back for breakfast, but this sort of winter morning isn't what you find in Fleet Street very readily. The air is so clear! And there are bushes with bright red fingers that poke at you as you walk. Rather like being beaten with birch twigs in Finland. But I felt I wanted to follow the path, and see where it went. Even Jane Cole would hardly refuse me a cup of coffee if I was late.

Surprisingly, the path left the woods after a short way and wound down through swampy grass to the drive we came up last night. I'd thought it would go out on the hill and climb away from the valley, and that I would get a view of the house from on high; but I see now that that would spoil the secrecy of Cressley. The fact is, you can't see the Cressley valley from anywhere. In the words of Muriel Cole, 'The buttercups were yellower because no one could see them. / The leaves on the maple took my last breath before they turned scarlet and fell.'

The path came out at the bottom of the drive, by the garden of the lodge cottage where Mr and Mrs Rees live. Thought I'd look in and say hello. It may turn out that Mrs Rees has to supply most of the 'atmosphere' for my *Clarion* piece, in a lilting Welsh brogue, no doubt.

As it turns out, Mrs Rees isn't from here at all. She and her husband both grew up in Ireland and she says they have no desire to go back there. Seems quite contented with the life at Cressley. Mr Rees wasn't around, but it was evident last night that he's extremely devoted etc. to the Cole family. Mrs Rees appears to be the same. She was like a photograph in a colour supplement, standing in a spotless front room and saying how Miss Cole had learnt a lot from her in the way of making pastry, and how she, Mrs Rees, could never understand why Miss Cole made those winy stews. Yes, everything's in its place in this strangest of all countries. I've always found the class system hard to grasp, and Richard makes the most of the fact that I only came over from Canada at the age of twenty.

'Every single comment you make on England, on the class system, on the political system, is pure *naïveté*,' he says.

That's why they hire me on the *Clarion*,' I reply, 'to get the fresh eye of an outsider.'

At this point Richard always snorts, and tries to tease me that John Carpenter (of all likely people!) is after me and that is why I'm employed there. Men still think deep down – female Prime Minister or no – that that can be the only reason why women are employed to do anything by men.

I tried Mrs Rees on the subject of Muriel Cole. Her buttony little eyes blinked at me quite hard. 'I get plenty of callers here at the lodge,' she said after a while. 'All wanting to know about Muriel Cole, Miss . . . ?'

'Catherine Treger.'

'Miss Treger. I always tell them the same thing. Twenty-one years is a long time. I always say, if Muriel Cole walked in here today, I wouldn't know her.'

'But you must have some memory of – well, what did you like least about her?'

Mrs Rees stared at me as if I had gone mad. I felt I had to explain I had come to Cressley by arrangement with Jane Cole, that I was a journalist on the *Clarion* and not a passing idolater – and hoped, as I did so, that Mrs Rees would relax a little. But the information seemed to make no difference to her at all. 'You're the first to ask me that,' she said after a pause. 'You mean, what didn't I like about her?' She laughed, with a malice that was a bit creepy in that spotless cottage where the Toby jugs and Mrs Rees's own rosy cheeks all contradict the idea of cruelty, or even humour. 'I was glad when she went. I shouldn't say this, but for twenty-one years the idea's been that she was hard done by – you know.' Mrs Rees lowered her voice. I thought I was getting a real scoop here, preferable to the possibly false one offered by Gertrud Ritchie last night – but all Mrs Rees added was: 'She wasn't my cup of tea. Everything had to be her way, you know the type. Do as you would be done by, that's what I say.'

And that was it. Nothing more could be got from her, other than details of domestic routine: that Muriel had disliked taking care of the house, had abominated housework, but had refused to let Jane Cole have full sway over linen cupboards and pantry. Mr and Mrs Rees had been 'living in' at the Grange, and there had been constant conflict. They had moved to the lodge shortly after Muriel's death: the implication was that the last trying years of Mrs Cole as an invalid had made the move a necessary one – if just to get some fresh air and distance between the Reeses and the big house.

By the time Mrs Rees had finished I felt quite sorry for Jane Cole, formidable and off-putting though the first impression of her might be. Muriel had been a domestic tyrant, and a sloppy one at that. It was only after I had said goodbye to Mrs Rees and was half running up the drive so as not to miss my coffee altogether, that I remembered who Muriel *had* been. A poet, an artist. Of course women like Mrs Rees, or Jane Cole herself for that matter, would resent someone so different from themselves, especially in the running of a house. And now I write this, I can't help smiling at the idea, so prevalent in my own circles, of housework shared by men and women being in any way relevant here. Jason Cole holding a Hoover would be the most ridiculous sight in the world. Oh dear, what am I really saying?

Breakfast was practically over by the time I went in to the refectory. After the brilliant light outside, I could hardly see, and it took Jane Cole's voice to guide me to the far end of the oak table, where the 'students' were crowded on to the bench.

'I don't believe you've met Jason,' Jane Cole said when I had squeezed myself in. A mug of tea was pushed down in my direction. (They don't go in for coffee here. Tragedy!) 'Jason, this is Catherine Treger from the *Clarion*.'

I wondered for a moment if Jason Cole would say something like, 'We may have seen each other,' or some facetious comment, but he made no reference to last night's spying on my part and looked me straight in the eye. I felt he knew very well, though, that I had seen him. He has a much more serious expression in public than when he's on his own – perhaps he knows that people watch him carefully. That must be the price of fame. Alone, his face is laughing and open – there's a kind of savage gaiety about it. But at the trestle table, with Jane Cole sitting over the teapot like some brooding squaw, and the 'students' nervous and tense, Jason could pass for a Senator: measured, pondering and somehow unbelievable.

Paul Ritchie was the first to break the awkward silence, which my arrival seemed only to have made worse. 'Catherine is going to explode the idea that creativity can be taught,' he said, leaning across the table to Jason. 'But

27

Jane will impart to her the magic secrets and she will leave a convert.'

Someone had to be facetious, I suppose. Joe Merton sniggered loudly. Pamela Wright gave a tight little smile, as if she had trained herself in advance to find anything intended to be amusing, just that. Lana shot me a horrified look which suggested I had come down to perform some sort of appendectomy on her creative muse. No reaction from Ken, as usual. (I'm more and more convinced he's on something pretty strong. Should Pamela Wright have brought him? Or is she trying to prove that opium can heighten the imagination?)

'I'm certainly not here to come to that conclusion,' I said. I am, of course, or that's what John Carpenter would like me to come up with, so I felt rather a fool. Also, for the first time for years, I blushed. Do I have some superstitious belief that poets are clairvoyant, that they can read what's going on in your mind? Because Jason Cole was staring at me as if he knew only too well the extent of the lie I'd just told.

'Catherine!' he said. He gave me a definitely strange look. I've heard, of course, that Jason Cole is a great charmer, but he certainly wastes less time than one would imagine. What did I feel then? Girlishly titillated is the best way of expressing it, I'm afraid.

Jane Cole jumped in after Jason said my name, and she did so with unexpected ferocity. 'Interviews start in thirty minutes,' she said. 'Names are on the rota in the hall. Two to clear breakfast, please.'

Is Jane Cole pathologically jealous, or what? Jason flicked a glance at her, rather like a horse brushing away a fly. He turned to look at me again. (But I don't want to get involved here. The impenetrable mysteries of the Coles . . . No, I like my job, and at all times when his family isn't over from Australia, I like Richard too.)

I decided the best thing to do was to volunteer to clear and wash up breakfast. I found myself in the small kitchen beside Lana Traill, the men having melted away like snow. From the refectory Jane Cole's voice boomed out again. 'Jason Cole will conduct interviews in the Martyr's Room. At the top of the small staircase here and three steps up to the left!'

The Martyr's Room! They certainly lay it on thick at Cressley. (Or 'Castaly', as Paul Ritchie muttered last night, explaining the fountain outside of the nymph Castalia as 'the spring with the power of inspiring with the gift of poetry those who drank from it'. Like many academics, Ritchie appears to have stunted his own creative processes.)

Let me see then. The landing from that small oak staircase in the refectory must join up with the locked-off end of the landing where I sleep. So possibly – in fact, probably – the Martyr's Room leads off Jason's room, which in turn adjoins mine.

As I was fixing the tape recorders, Pamela Wright, my neighbour on the other side, put her head round the door. She asked if she could borrow my toothpaste, as she had left hers behind. I don't think she saw the cassette, or at least I hope she didn't, as I don't particularly want everyone to know what I'm about to do.

11.15 a.m.

This has been such a strange and disconcerting morning that I'm quite glad John Carpenter rang (just as I was going to begin spying) and told me he wants a bigger piece, and sooner than the original deadline. Normally I'd curse him for it. But it may help to put my mind in order if I have to concentrate on the piece. Not that the various quotes from sources such as the poet Adrian Mitchell, who calls for 'an end to these ridiculous courses', seem to have any bearing whatsoever on life at Cressley Grange.

After John's call, I went back up to my room, crept through the door in the wall by the side of the bed, and went through into Jason's room, which was of course empty. It crossed my mind for a mad moment that the original M S of this newly discovered novel of Muriel Cole's might be lying on the desk or somewhere obvious, and I might copy out a quick passage for the *Clarion*. But there was no sign of anything as bulky as that. I didn't stop by the great untidy pile of letters and – I imagine – first drafts of poems, because I could hear Jason's voice on the other side of the wall. I was right: there *is* a connection between Jason's room and the Martyr's Room. A battered-looking red curtain against the far wall conceals a short flight of whitewashed, very ancient-looking steps. I have to admit I felt quite nervous as I went over the creaking boards to the steps, and when I bumped into the drum and it gave a sort of muffled *poing*! I nearly screamed. Matters weren't helped by the tribal masks, which seemed to watch me with malevolence as I went about my trespassing. One of them, just above the drum, had the pure, narrow features of Jason, and I had a horrible feeling that behind the blank, slit eyes, his eyes were looking contemptuously out at me.

As it happened, the was a perfect small platform at the foot of the steps, and a keyhole in the door so large that I could actually see the back of Jason's head, and a part of his interviewee's face as well. I could even hang the cassette from the door handle! Apart from the extreme cold and damp of the stone under my knees, it was the most ideal spying terrain I've ever come across.

30

The person facing Jason wasn't a 'student' at all, but Gertrud Ritchie. And she must have just arrived, because she seemed agitated and breathless. By the look of things Jason wasn't too pleased at seeing her, either.

JASON: I *was* surprised to see you this morning, Gertrud. I thought Paul was coming on his own.

GERTRUD: I couldn't help it, do I have to tell you that you haven't answered *any* of my letters?

JASON: I've been very busy. Really . . . I don't know why I do it. *Laughs*. Up and down the country. Wearing down the hills.

GERTRUD: But you're touring your own kingdom, Jason. An ancient king, before the mean Christian spirit came to crush the land . . .

JASON: Don't forget you're in the Martyr's Room, Gertrud. They might not like to hear you speak like that.

GERTRUD: You're angry with me. Still angry with me, I can tell.

JASON: Look, Gertrud. I've a lot of papers to go through and I've interviews with the students here.

GERTRUD: Do I really not mean anything to you any more, Jason?

JASON: We'll have a drink in the pub over the weekend. Promise.

GERTRUD: Bastard! Muriel was right about you. Well, I'll tell you that I've rumbled it all at last. I know now! I have proof!

JASON: What the hell are you talking about?

GERTRUD: 'The Revellers', Jason. And I even said as much to that little journalist girl last night –

31

At this point Jason got up and physically bundled Gertrud Ritchie out of the room. His legs came right up against the keyhole as she lunged at him and pushed him backwards and then everything jigged about so it was impossible to tell what was happening. Finally the door banged and he came back to sit at the desk. He was out of breath. He drummed his fingers on the desk top in a kind of insistent, loud rhythm which almost made me afraid I might go into a trance and be found years later, a skeleton holding a cassette recorder and grinning.

A knock on the door. Jason's fingers came down with a thud on the leather. I recognized Lana's voice – you'd know the whining, self-pitying tone anywhere.

JASON: Please sit down. Like to show me some of your work?

LANA: I came here to be in the place Muriel lived in. Miss Cole said all the students had to come and see you, but I didn't know it was compulsory.

JASON: It isn't. But this isn't a course for people to study the work of Muriel Cole, either. You might waste less of your time and ours if you went home, Lana.

LANA: I only brought the automatic writing with me. The prose poem isn't ready yet.

JASON: Well, I'll look at that, then.
    After silent reading:

JASON: That's quite promising, Lana. Have you been helped before by anyone?

LANA: I'm helped by the spirit of Muriel. She comes to me at night – she did almost all of the automatic writing, I'm sure of that –

JASON: My next interview is on the way now. Will you give this note to Jane Cole, please?

LANA: I had to see The Old House. I dreamt it often and then it was just as I expected when I got here . . .

Poor Jason Cole! What a morning! He had to practically throw Lana Traill out of his room as well, except she was obviously more frightened of him than Gertrud had been. No wonder it's called the Martyr's Room: Jason pays more heavily than one would imagine for his legendary fame.

My cassette very thoughtfully ran out at this point, and before I had time to reload, Joe Merton came into the room. As usual I saw just about a third of his face, then there was a slice of violently coloured tweed jacket and a white folder, which I realized was shaking in the poor sod's hands. A keyhole-shaped portion of Jason's narrow elegant hand went out to take it.

When I look back on that exchange I wish more than ever that the recorder had been working. There was a silence while Jason read the offered poems. Then he leant back in his chair until he was nearly falling back on my door again. The front legs of the chair reared up like a horse. I remember thinking Jason looked like some fantastic Mexican adventurer, or a picador, high on his mount above the cowering (but basically arrogant) apprentice artist.

'Do you want me to tell you the truth straight?' Jason said.

Even where I was sitting, this sounded ominous. Is this the way 'the skill that cannot be taught' *is* taught by those who believe in it? I couldn't of course see Jason's face, but if I'd been on the receiving end, I would have felt like running for it while there was still time.

'You think they're . . .' poor Joe Merton began.

'Give it up,' Jason Cole said.

'But . . .'

33

'More people write poetry than read it in this country.' Jason had brought the front legs of his chair down and he was sitting right back in it now, like a friar, with hands folded over a non-existent paunch. 'But even if you were prepared to educate yourself, which I can see from these that you are not, you lack any ear, any talent whatsoever. You're wasting your time.'

The extraordinary part was that Joe Merton obviously didn't believe what he had just heard. Maybe the shock was too great. His face loomed up over the desk – now I see why Jason set himself back like that, he must know how to prepare himself for the counter-attack – and he said, 'I don't contaminate my art with the dead culture of the past.'

Yes, that's what he said. He had moved his face over to the side a little so I had the middle of it in front of me – a nose coloured as red, white and blue as the Union Jack, by winter colds and the present agitation, and some yellow spots that looked like miniature cup-cakes on a red and slightly unshaven chin.

'Homer,' Jason said very quietly. 'Chaucer. Shakespeare.' I couldn't help smiling at this. No doubt Jason is a fine actor. Because Joe Merton stared at him as if the familiar names were going to hypnotize him – and Jason rolled them round his tongue, slowly, wonderingly, a man tasting the finest wine on earth, where each sip is better and fresher than the last.

'*Paradise Lost*,' Jason said. 'Joe Merton. Ah. I see what you mean. How foolish of me.'

Joe Merton's face rose from the keyhole and was rapidly followed by a piece of sweater framed on one side with tweed jacket. Then came the groin, in dirty jeans. Steps went slowly and heavily to the door.

'Thank you.' Joe Merton's voice was thick. 'Mr Cole.' The door shut with a bang. There had been a distinct

34

note of sarcasm in the 'Mr Cole': is it conceivable that Joe Merton still considers himself a genius? But to leave an interview like that with the conviction that you, Joe Merton, are right and an expert like Jason Cole is wrong, is near to insanity. Perhaps I've exaggerated, though – the note of sarcasm was probably the only thing the wretched guy could think up.

I now have to relate an unpleasant experience. In the long silence that followed I tried to reload the cassette recorder. I did it, or so I thought, noiselessly. But Jason must have the eyes and hearing of a wild animal. He swivelled with astonishing speed – now I look back on it he was like a cowboy in a Western, ludicrously quick on the draw – and he stared straight at the keyhole. That tiny click, from a spool in a case behind an oak door, had put every one of his instincts on full alert.

I know I shouldn't have done what I did. But in this profession you might as well be hung for a sheep as a lamb. When I'd stopped blushing from having my eye caught (and that's the silly part, Jason had seen only my eye while I had seen a good deal more of him), I moved back up the stone steps and I deliberately made it sound like a graceless person on tiptoe, someone trying to be quiet who didn't know how. Then I crouched at the top of the steps and waited.

There was silence from the Martyr's Room. My heart nearly missed a beat because at one point a chair scraped back over stone flags, and I thought Jason was about to come in pursuit of me. But he must have been stretching his legs – the chair was pulled forward again and at the same time, the door opened and closed.

I turned the mike as far in the direction of the last step as it would go, and inched my way down on my bottom until I was three steps from the keyhole. To go nearer would have been madness – I felt very conscious of Jason being conscious of me, of his wondering whether I had gone or stayed.

At first I thought the person who had come in was Gertrud again, reappearing to remonstrate with Jason over his heartless behaviour. Then I found I couldn't place the voice at all. Was it Jane Cole perhaps? It soon became clear, though, that Jason wasn't on familiar terms with the woman. He sounded polite, and rather tired – maybe these Joe Merton-type confrontations really take it out of him.

JASON: Do sit down. It's . . .

The mike didn't pick up here very well. Judging by the movements and more chairs being pulled about, there were two people in there with Jason now.

JASON: Of course. Pamela Wright.
PAMELA: And this is Ken. We brought some of his early poems, written while he was still at Turlington Green, and some of his recent work, since he's been at the factory –
JASON: Yes, yes. Ken, would you like to pull up a chair – that small one over by the window –
PAMELA: It's so fascinating to come here, Mr Cole. You know, on the way down in the train I couldn't help reading 'The Old House' again. It's such a moving poem, I find. And Cressley does have a –
JASON: Would you mind being silent while I read these poems, Mrs Wright? Thank you.

Another of Jason's reading silences. This time I felt quite nervous, in case the hapless Ken got the Joe Merton treatment. How would he handle it? Perhaps it was Pamela who had insisted he come down here in the first place, and

36

he couldn't care less. But then with people on drugs – and after another look at him at breakfast I *know* he must be – not caring is what they're taking the drugs for. It's a vicious circle.

JASON: These are good, Ken. I like them.
PAMELA: No! I told you, Ken! I told you!
JASON: The more recent work is better than the early poems–
PAMELA: Oh, I don't agree! I'm sorry to butt in here –
JASON: Excuse me. Ken, what you want to do is to concentrate on the imagery here. As you know, on the Saturday of the course, each student goes off and writes on his own. Don't try and rush things. I'll look forward to seeing your work tomorrow morning. Take as much time this evening as you like.

I wonder if anyone is ever going to hear Ken speak. Pamela Wright burbled some more, Jason showed them out, and the teacher went off with her silent poet to search for a suitable place for creation (I can see that sharing a room with Joe Merton wouldn't be exactly inspiring). I crept through the red curtain – into Jason's room – ran to my door without catching the eye of the pre-Columbian masks – and here I am. Luckily Jason didn't leave the Martyr's Room via the stairs to his own room. He must have gone down to the refectory, because there's no sound from him next door, even if I turn my electric portable off and sit in the silence after the hum.

So to sum up. I'm glad Ken has been given the holy seal of approval. But how can Jason Cole tell so quickly whether a young poet is good, or 'promising', or not? I suppose I'm not really the person to come down here, from that point of view, because most contemporary poetry seems so bad to me anyhow. Prose, I think, is far

37

more interesting – even the despised journalism is often better than a pretentious, meaningless poem. Yet there's great reverence for poets, perhaps because they're thought to be the only people, in the materialistic society we live in, who are doing something uncommercial.

As for whether the skill can be taught – if I'm able to snoop at the meeting between Jason and Ken, after today's lines have been written, I may get an idea of the process. Certainly Ken should feel encouraged. (In fact, so should Lana, but she's such a silly little goose that she puts her obsessions far above her talents.) I wouldn't like to be Joe Merton, though. Or was Jason really being kind? Is it better to be told you're no bloody good – then, instead of battering your head against a brick wall, you go off and do something else and enjoy it, even? I don't know that Jason wasn't right after all.

Later

Another half-hour or so before my interview with Jane Cole. It's odd how one's mood can change: half an hour ago I was decrying the charms of poetry. Now, sitting in this room with its odd, uneven walls and white-washed sills that are high and deep, I find I'm thinking about Muriel again, and the undoubted power her poems once exercised over me. I think of her childhood, the tragedy for her when her mother and sister and she had to come back from Greece for ever – and her father didn't come too. To the grim north of England, where Muriel's mother's family lived. Is it the break from family warmth and intimacy, perhaps, to something more aloof, more distant, which takes place around the age of eleven –

Muriel's age at the time of the break – that is summed up in the transition from beautiful, golden Greece to the harsh realities of a northern Quaker circle? And Muriel's mother was ill so often – as in 'Shells':

> Shells – in a winter sickroom –
> Lips gaping at a grim scene
> of white over white trees
> and a grudging strip of brown

I remember that. And her mother painting her nails – 'a conch-glow – ten moons half rising'. Then, as the winter grows more grim and 'The hills are scandalized/Crows riot in snow and foul the track./But from the shells – hot seas – the Cyclades –/ burst from a sky pulled back and back.' I suppose the dream of the shells bursting with life and colour is common to young girls: a dream of their own bright future, combined with guilt and sorrow over an ageing mother. I think of my own mother, and her rapid decline, after she and my father were divorced. Richard has never understood why I minded that so much.

There, I'm nearly in tears. Muriel has done it again. But we all need people like Muriel, I think. It's so easy to live on the surface. With a job like mine, horrifically easy. What moved you in adolescence seems a long way away. Muriel is a sacrifice – a scapegoat: by her minding, by the sharpness of her feelings, she can pull one into the things that really mattered, and still do. And it's not surprising one should feel this way again – this was her home, after all. I can remember now, from 'The Old House', which both Lana and Pamela Wright mentioned:

> I confess, I confess.
> I *am* in love with The Old House
> It's either me or my grandmother,

it doesn't matter which.
And all I want are the women
in blue-grey, and the trees in silver-grey.

Poor Muriel! It seems she wasn't popular even here, if
Mrs Rees is anything to go by. Perhaps her sense of her
impending death, which was too much of a tragedy for
those close to her to bear, became simply irritating?

For Muriel always had that sense. Long before the
accident which gave her such pain, against which she
resorted to larger and larger doses of morphine. When she
was still young – before she met Jason, even – when she
was beginning to get to know other young poets in London
and at Oxford, she spoke often and intensely of the first
time she tried to commit suicide – aged eleven, after being
separated from Greece and her father. She saw her father
as the sea, which is strange when one thinks for how many
centuries the sea has been woman, pulled by the moon.
But the fierce, bright blue Aegean was what she lost – her
father the sea, and her mother country.

> She threw me back, gasping
> The sea accommodates me,
> nine fathoms down
> black as a night without a moon.

Muriel tried to drown herself in the mill pond in the
northern village she hated. She was pulled out just in time.
And although she didn't actually make the attempt again
until the night, here at Cressley, when pain and the impossible conflicts of her nature drove her to the act, she was
as obsessed by suicide as were Anne Sexton and Sylvia
Plath. Something in those women made them see life as
untenable, unliveable – but one must say, in all honesty, that
they did a lot to change the expectations of women. The

absolute hopelessness of women's situation thirty years ago doesn't look as if it could ever be repeated. One ought to feel unbounded gratitude to Muriel. Why is it, then, that one feels a reluctance about her – as those near her evidently did? Is it simply a dislike for illness and pain?

The shelves here, under the sills in Muriel's room, are crowded with volumes of her poetry, and of Jason's. Just opened a battered-looking copy of *Stultifera Navis*. 'To Jason. With all my love. Muriel.' And, surprisingly, a volume of Jason Cole's latest poems – *E O S* (1985).

I must admit I had a funny feeling in the pit of my stomach when I read the inscription in Jason's volume. 'For Muriel. Love always, Jason.'

What can this mean?

Also have to admit I've taken a drop of Scotch from my provident store – feel rather shaken. Everyone assumed that this 'irritating' quality of Muriel's – her self-pity, her plangency and of course her constant pain alternating with being in a drugged state – had alienated Jason from her totally. It was even said that Jason had girls then, who came to Cressley – and who could blame him, in such appalling circumstances? But now it seems that Jason has never stopped loving Muriel. Even inscribing his latest volume to her so many years after her death, and leaving it in her room, next to her own work.

I have to wonder why I should feel both attacked and depressed by this. Am I already under the spell of Jason Cole? I'm behaving as if I were jealous!

It may be Jason's recent and deep affirmation of the Christian faith which has made him love his wife again. Remorse at feelings that went elsewhere, maybe, and caused her additional pain. A golden memory of the early days of the marriage. Similar to Hardy's passionate revival of feeling for his poor wife Emma after her death. It

41

must be that. There's something in it which turns the stomach. And I feel deflated, as well.

What do I think of this last, Christian phase of the poet who would once have felt unbearably cramped in either formal metre or religious symbolism? I don't know enough about poetry to know, but opening the book at the title poem, I feel it may be relevant to quote it in the piece for the *Clarion*, contrasting the path Muriel Cole took before her death and the way Jason Cole is going now.

EOS
by Jason Cole (1984)

Mother of life, you dive into the pool
and sleep. Stones in a lost inventory
of monsters once the lords of ancient rule
Move deep in your green sovereignty.

You are the bringer of our every spring,
you are the ending of the winter's kiss.
From your green pool an oceanic dream
enfolds our wonder at the promising.

The trees are crimson with the stain of crime.
Thorns on the cross atone what you have done.
Rising, the stones set in your gaudy crown
and tilt at winter's long-forgotten name.

After the fall, no reason and no shame
deplore His absence and His late return.

It all seems rather sad to me. Yet Jason doesn't seem a depressed man, and he's certainly far from one's idea of a monk! I'm being too naïve, I expect, in linking an artist's work with his personality. This type of poem may be a way for Jason to relieve his melancholy, an expiation, in a sense, for the past.

Must go along to Jane Cole now. I don't feel, somehow, that I'm going to get very far with her on any subject – Muriel, or subsidies to the arts, or whatever. She's even more of a mask than her cousin. I wonder, dare I ask her to show me the novel – I shall, of course, and she will refuse – and dare I ask her about Gertrud and her wild accusations? Difficult to imagine, while on such firmly marked-out Cole territory, saying: 'I was told last night by Mrs Ritchie, Miss Cole, that Mr Cole's most celebrated poem, "The Revellers" was, in fact, the trigger of his wife's suicide. Can you corroborate this?'

1.30 p.m.

How am I ever going to manage to write this piece? In the past ten minutes, phone calls from Richard *and* John Carpenter. Richard to say that Melanie and family have arrived. 'I put Melanie in the spare room. No, it's *not* perfectly easy for her to ring the Fletchers and go and stay there. No, I didn't say I was expecting her to stay right over Christmas. I've ordered the turkey, by the way. We'll get a fresher one if we order direct from this place in Norfolk, the mail-order place. Melanie says what do you want for Christmas?'

It would take years of expensive analysis, I fear, to work out why that conversation has made me so angry. How typical of Richard to move in Melanie just because my back is turned. He goes on sickeningly enough about

43

missing his family since they emigrated to Australia – but when they do come they sulk at each other all the time, and Melanie will just sit there while Richard occasionally addresses a sarcastic remark to her. Only she's not going to, because I want her out before I get back. And the turkey! Ordering it early – how unbearably prissy – I feel as if he was shoving it down my throat. I'm amazed not to hear there's a leak in the roof too; Richard would so enjoy clambering about on the wet tiles and then calling to tell me about it.

John Carpenter in his own way was just as bad. The piece to be in by 17 December now – that's only a week from today! Demands I get a chunk from the newly discovered novel, at all costs. Has a large photograph of Jason and Muriel together – says it'll make a good spread. The thought of the photograph is depressing, somehow.

The trouble with both calls is that they've dislocated me – or that's what it feels like. I'm oddly *settled* here. It must be the house, and Muriel's room with the odd proportions that seem to alter to fit your state or mood – anyway, I don't feel drawn in the slightest to London and the flat (I won't be able to get Melanie out, of course: once in, she's in), or to the office and the cardboard coffee. Who would be drawn to that combination? But here, one gets a sudden flash of what a different kind of life would be like. A serious life, like Jason's – and the beauty of the country, waiting for the flowers to come up in spring . . .

Later

Going by the above I must have been doing some automatic writing myself. Follows: a quick record of the last few hours. It looks dismally as if I'm going to have to start the actual piece here, if it has to be in by the 17th. Don't like writing on the spot, it takes away the sense of distance. But it won't be fun at home. Melanie always insists on a 'reunion dinner' when she sees me again, and I end up having to cook it. Just hearing her stumbling about in the kitchen is a thousand times worse than making a whole week of dinners oneself.

Jane Cole – I hardly know how to begin.

At least I think I've got the hang of the interior of Cressley now. Jane's room is in a kind of bridge between the two main landings. She told me how to get there, and I found it quite easily. It's a big room, with large, square windows overlooking the front garden, the fountain and the drive. (Odd, I'd have thought she'd choose the back of the house, it's more *her* with some of the rooms long and low, like Turkish rooms, and great fireplaces knocked into the walls under fat planks of wood.) In the front, maybe, she can spy on whoever is coming to the house.

It wouldn't be surprising to find that Jane Cole actually fires from her window at unwelcome visitors! I've never seen such a collection of antique firearms – and swords too – the walls are covered in them. With all this musketry, it comes as a slight shock to see a very feminine bed over in the corner: four-poster, rose-sprigged muslin curtains – even a strawberry-coloured quilt and a battered teddy bear!

45

Before I had a chance to push open the door further, though, I realized Jane Cole wasn't alone in her 'boudoir', and I closed it again quickly. Two voices – one of them was quite loud, and with a marked foreign accent. Gertrud was up to her trouble again. I must say, that woman could only politely be described as a pain in the neck. I wonder that the Coles allow her to come to Cressley. But old friendships like that always astonish me. What's in it for any of them?

'Yes,' the foreign voice came through the door. 'I mean it, Jane.'

'Don't be so idiotic,' Jane's voice came back.

'Jane! I have decided to tell all, and I mean it!'

'The best thing you can possibly do is to go home and have a rest.'

'I'll show her the proof!'

'Now – look –'

'And you recognize –'

The door was suddenly pulled open. But not before – I was already so intrigued by the exchange that I'm sure I couldn't have made a mistake – Gertrud Ritchie, in a loud, dramatic whisper, said my name, 'Catherine!' in that guttural way of hers, making a 'Katrine' or 'Katerina' of me. Then Jane Cole was standing face to face with me. I tried my best to look embarrassed. Most people never know how hardened journalists become in these situations.

'I have an appointment – so sorry if I'm early –'

'Could you kindly come back in ten minutes? There's been a slight hold-up here.' Jane blinked into my eyes as she spoke and then the door shut as fast as it had opened. I even heard a key in the lock!

This time, though, I couldn't hang around in the corridor: it was too risky. If someone saw – I'd be asked to leave – no piece for the *Clarion* and possibly no job by the New Year. I went back along the bridge towards my bedroom landing, then decided to slip down into the hall, and through into the sitting-room. I was looking for a writer in the grip of creative inspiration – a quick interview with the inspired one could fill in the time nicely.

There was no one around. Budding writers must be like nesting birds: they build as far out of sight as possible. It was probably silly of me to imagine all the 'students' sitting in a polite row on a couch in front of the log fire, notebooks on their laps and pencils at the ready. Hasn't one heard only too often how isolated 'the writer's lot' must be. And who would want to start writing with a portrait of Muriel Cole hanging directly opposite!

So I sat down myself. Thoughts that went through my head, as I waited, were mainly on the Gertrud scandal and whether it was exploding now in Jane Cole's well-armed room. Does Gertrud really want to ruin Jason's career? If so, is it simply revenge for having been slighted? How does she know the famous poem was the cause of Muriel's death? I must interview her and get to the bottom of this. Or is she blackmailing the Coles?

It all seems a bit unlikely. Perhaps it's really to do with artistic integrity – not a commodity I'm well up on, surrounded daily as I am by a company of hacks. Perhaps Gertrud simply wants Jason and Jane to admit privately that Muriel had to forgo her own ambition to enable her husband to write 'The Revellers'. She's proved it, and she wants them to speak the truth. But then, why should she have offered the 'scoop' last night? It looks as if something not entirely connected with integrity is going on here.

The worst part, I suppose, is that 'The Revellers' was

the confirmation of Jason Cole's poetic voice. To reveal a sad story at the heart of this most savage – and pagan – of lyrics would be to alter his identity, somehow. For one has to face facts – there hasn't been the popular liking or the critical esteem for the recent, religious poems. 'The Revellers' *is* Jason Cole.

As I was sitting, increasingly drowsy in the heat of the log fire, and saying the lines to myself, and reflecting (I'm sorry to say) that I'd rather Gertrud got nowhere with her horrible scoop, I heard a rustling sound from the far end of the sitting-room. I don't know why, but I felt a sudden fear. It was a primal fear, like sensing, in a jungle, the presence of something alive in the trees. I suppose I must have thought I was utterly alone – maybe, looking back on it, I was ashamed of the thoughts I was having – and when one discovers someone else is there, one always feels they've heard one's thoughts as clearly as if they were spoken aloud.

There's a piano at the far end of the room, and beyond it a low bench covered in the rough peasant cloth Jane Cole clearly likes to strew around Cressley. The top of a head just showed over the piano. Lower down, framed by piano legs, a pair of crossed knees were visible and two hands shuffling sheets of paper. The rustling lost its jungle associations, but I wish I could say I stopped feeling frightened. If anything, the sense of danger grew.

Joe Merton rose slowly and edged his way along the bench. One hand appeared to be stroking the piano as he went – or, the unpleasant thought struck, it was *groping*, for he certainly walked like a blind man – and the other clenched the sheaf of papers.

What I remember best about the next minute or so are the eyes of Muriel Cole. In my dread at the approach of Joe Merton I must have glanced at the portrait above the mantelpiece (like gazing at the stained-glass window above an altar, perhaps, or the effigy of a saint, in desperate hope for succour); and having done so, I found I was attached to that face in the most extraordinary way. I literally couldn't take my eyes off it. And it seemed – as I was in a state of what the Victorians termed 'heightened sensibility' – that Muriel Cole couldn't take her eyes off me. Those black, oval eyes burned straight through into some inner part of myself that I haven't been in touch with for so long I'd forgotten it was there. I felt guilt, and a kind of resigned feeling which isn't 'me' at all. The eyes seemed reproachful, too. She knew I'd been remembering lines of Jason's poem and hoping he would be protected from obloquy. Already – against her – I was on his side.

By the time Muriel's eyes had finally moved from my face, Joe Merton was standing by the settee. I knew he was there, of course. The fear I'd had in his presence had changed now – dangerously – to the resignation which seemed to emanate from Muriel. I can't honestly say I know what it's like to be close to death, but I could swear that moment was the nearest I've come to it. The resignation was so great it was like a paralysis. And it was as much as I could do to keep my eyes open: they were heavy, as if I had just been drugged.

'I'd like to show you my latest work,' Joe Merton said.

'I'd be very interested to see it,' I replied.

It was difficult to take in that this matter-of-fact exchange had taken place. Joe Merton, who was unpleasant to look at when 'normal', was quite horrifying in his present state. He looked, I thought, like one of those drawings by schizophrenics: face an angry red and subtly the wrong shape, as if someone had squeezed and pinched it, hair sticking up, and wild eyes, flecked with yellow and red, that seemed to have lost most of the pupils, leaving a kind of mad-dog look. He was tilting heavily to one side as he stood, like a man on a ship in high seas.

'Do you mind if I sit here?' he said.

I don't know how I got through those minutes, or how many of them there were. All I know is that I must decide in the very near future whether to go to Jane Cole and tell her what I fear. I should, of course, have told her before now. Something held me back . . . what was it . . . a sort of pity for the poor bloke, I suppose.

Joe Merton said he'd written the long poem that very morning, after his interview with Jason Cole.

'How did that go?' I asked nervously. He had pushed the pages into my hand – I hated holding them. I even thought a bad smell was coming off them! (Another symptom of heightened sensibility?)

'Fine,' Joe Merton said. 'Great.'

I looked down nervously at Joe Merton's 'poem'. But his face, or the after-image of it, kept coming between me and the page. Anyone can see he's in very serious trouble indeed.

> The knife
> The knife hits the bone
> The scream comes out from behind its curtain
> > of blood,
> your entrails gnawed by carrion.
> Cole man! Killer of life,
> my hands on your white breath
> and your guts lumping, crawling over stone.

And so on. And so on. My first reaction was to feel sick. But at least the nausea took the place of the feeling of fatality. I got to my feet just as Joe Merton's physical presence and literary emanations were about to overpower me completely.

'Very interesting, Joe. As you know, I'm only a journalist, and no great judge of –'

Joe Merton tittered. He rose, too, and put his face a disgusting two inches from mine. There were specks of foam on his lips – he was like a parody of a madman.

'Ole King Cole,' he said. 'He'd better enjoy the next world as much as he hopes he's going to, with all that religious shit.'

'You don't like the relig–' I began.

'Because that's where he's going,' Joe said. 'Will he be a king there? Ha! I wonder! Because I know he's not going where he thinks he's going. He's going to the other place!'

Why didn't I take Joe's poems and march straight off to Jane Cole with them? Instead, I said: 'Why don't you let me have the poem for an hour or two, Joe – I'd like to print some of it in the article. I really do think it's excellent.'

Joe Merton grinned, if that's how you describe the foam-flecked lips struggling about in his face, not unlike the entrails on which he dwells so gloatingly. 'You want to use some of it?' he said.

'I have to square all my pieces with the editor, of course. But I think it would be int–'

Then the most horrible thing imaginable happened: Joe Merton seized me, pressed those wriggling worms on to my lips, and forced my head right back. I struggled, but he was very strong: he had me in a vice.

The door of the sitting room opened. Jason Cole and Jane came in together.

I still find it upsetting to write about this. What must they think?

As far as I remember, the Coles were having a low, almost whispered conversation. It sounded very urgent. Perhaps Jane was telling him about Gertrud? At any rate, they stopped suddenly when they saw us in the middle of the room. Jason said – and it was particularly humiliating:

'I'm so sorry.'

I don't know why, but his good-humoured acceptance of the situation was the last straw. Couldn't he *see* I was struggling to get away? I let out the most awful scream, half of which got muffled on Joe Merton's scratchy shoulder – but the other half made the message clear.

It was Jane Cole who ran to my rescue. Her powerful arms soon tore Joe Merton away from me. I'm ashamed to say I was sobbing. Not the emancipated woman at all. Though after the last rape programme on TV I did take a couple of judo lessons – then gave up.

'We'll talk about this later,' Jane said to Joe Merton.

She practically shoved him out of the room. As he ran out into the stone-flagged hall and up the stairs to his landing, he made a terrible noise, like a chicken having its neck wrung. Now I look back on it, he's obviously in a dangerous psychotic state – I must go and show these poems to Jane. And she should ring a doctor. But all I did at the time was shove the offending poems into my jacket pocket – as if I'd written them! – and hope Jason, having seen me and Joe Merton in an apparent clinch, wouldn't think I was an easy lay who had come down to Cressley to get a bit on the side.

Jason didn't seem to be thinking along those lines or any other remotely connected with them. He was pacing at the far end of the room, where French windows lead out on to a short lawn, then to a cobbled courtyard and the barn where Lana and the Ritchies sleep, and he seemed deep in thought, almost frighteningly so. A man with the concentration of Jason Cole is literally 'undisturbable' in that state, and I saw Jane glance quickly at him, decide to leave him to his thoughts and then nod at me to follow her up to the interview.

I must confess I left the room reluctantly. If Jason could have looked up once! But, as before, he had caught me, briefly, in a compromising situation and then had looked away again. It's upsetting to be seen falsely, and then ignored. But – an uncomfortable thought – was I really seen falsely? After all, it *was* me on each occasion – spying on him and, perhaps you could say, enticing Joe Merton with my inquisitiveness, which the poor wretch was bound to confuse with genuine interest.

It suits Jason to be 'deep in thought' though. His dark head pushes forward, and with his high cheekbones and glinting eyes he reminds me of the portrait Sargent did of Robert Louis Stevenson – a pacing, glittering man in a room.

Jane must have sensed my feelings, because after we'd gone halfway up the stairs to my landing, and crossed the bridge to her quarters, she turned and smiled at me. 'Jason's in the throes of a new, long poem,' she said. 'He probably seems a little distracted to you. But I'm sure you'll be able to have a chat later. Quite sure.'

It occurs to me here that I haven't really described Jane Cole for *Clarion* readers. She's what you might call 'composed'. But now I look at the word, I wonder what I mean by it. Composed of a lot of different people, perhaps, she doesn't seem quite *real*. None of this can I put in the piece, of course: I'll stick to 'soft-voiced'.

The door was opened, and Jane Cole put her head round it, as if expecting someone to be there; then, after a thorough inspection, she pushed it wider and went in.

'Is it a long poem in the *E O S* tradition?' I asked carefully.

Perhaps Jane had been wondering if Gertrud were still in her room, waiting to sabotage our interview with her explosive news about 'The Revellers'.

'Long for him,' Jane answered with a rare smile. It really is a remarkable face – eyes expressionless, bones high and narrow – and a smile as sweet and childish as the rose four-poster amongst the guns and pistols on her walls.

'Many of these are Byron's – and his soldiers', in use at Missolonghi,' Jane said when she saw me looking round. 'I'm a Byronomane, you know.'

'Really.' I couldn't think of anything to say. Maybe living with Jason Cole and his powerful poetic personality was too overwhelming, and a rival interest had to be found.

'And that's my favourite picture of him,' Jane said. 'Doesn't he look nice?'

I said he did. The picture in question, a miniature, was framed in silver and stood on an elegant French table under a display of swords. I rather wished Jane Cole wouldn't keep referring to him in the present tense – but I suppose that's the order of the day at Cressley Institute of Creative Writing: a poet is immortal, and like the elements he will return forever.

'I was wondering . . . if it would be at all possible . . . to see the novel,' I said.

Jane Cole had her back to me. She was standing under the swords and taking one more look at the poet who broke more hearts than any other poet before or since. I heard her sigh. Perhaps she's secretly in love with her cousin? Transferring it all on to Lord Byron. But this will get me nowhere. She did at least surprise me by nodding her head at once and turning with another smile – a decorous one this time – and indicating a seat. I sat down on a gold chair with a cherry velvet cushion, near the window looking out over the drive.

'I'll give you the manuscript,' she said. 'Only until you leave of course –'

'Of course,' I said. (I can hardly believe my luck – I'll take quite a long extract and that will shorten the piece.)

'It's a fascinating book. But first and foremost, Muriel was a poet.'

I really thought I was getting somewhere. I asked Jane Cole if she would mind a tape recorder listening in on us.

'No, go ahead,' she said.

I suppose I should have noticed then how abstracted, dreamy, Jane Cole was at that moment. I still can't decide whether that's her way of dealing with awkwardnesses – to go half asleep, like a cat – or if the result of her doing that made me handle the interview in an absurd, crass way. No. She wasn't going to give anything in the first place. She simply led me on.

Q: I read that Muriel Cole wrote the novel in the last year of her life. What – er – what was she *like* in that year?

A: You see – why we have to sit by the window is that on Saturdays you can sometimes get the wrong kind of people coming here.

Q: We know Muriel Cole was in pain as a result of her motor accident. Can you tell me how it happened?

A: There. No, it isn't. I thought that woman on the lawn at the front of the house was the same as the young lady I had to expel last week. *She* was from California, she said. I pointed out that hardly gave her the right to walk into the house uninvited.

55

Laughter from Jane Cole; strained laughter from me.

Q: Muriel skidded on a roundabout and swerved into a lorry –

A: Muriel Cole had a self-destructive nature.

Q: You mean, she deliberately –

A: People are guided by their destinies. Muriel had a particularly strong demon. Who knows what it said to her then? *Laughs.* Anyway, she was a rotten driver.

Q: But she was in pain all the time she was writing the novel. In your opinion, did the morphine it's said she took at that time – er – affect the writing?

A: Have you ever been to Greece, Catherine?

Q: Greece –?

A: Have you seen that intense, blue sky? That's where Muriel spent her early years. Beautiful. Where Byron died. Beautiful. No drug could compare with the strength of that honey smell from the Attic mountains . . . you remember, she said: 'Blue / Fell to the ocean lip / And holding them apart, one blue, cloud-lidded eye.' Muriel's memories were stronger than anyone's. Even Jason's. We don't know enough about memory yet, Catherine.

Q: So the novel is a dream work –

A: Why would they pay over a million if it was just another drug trip? Here. See what you think of it, anyway.

Q: Thank you so much. I didn't mean to – I'm sure I wouldn't be a judge of these things anyway. But while we're on the subject of money . . .

A: Are we?

Q: I wanted to ask you about the grant you receive for the running of Cressley Grange. In your opinion, has a sufficient proportion of students benefited in a concrete way from the course to justify the outlay?

A: Concrete? We don't go in for that sort of poetry here, you know. *Laughs.* Though I'm fond of George Pendy. Do you know him?

Q: One of the Liverpool . . .

A: Yes, yes. Catherine, I can only say that we are *not* here to turn out competitive, ambitious people – the kind of people who – who go into journalism. I beg your pardon. But you must ask yourself, how long is it since you have looked at a tree?

Q: A tree?

A: Really looked at a tree. A long time, I suspect. The people here are learning to do that. A poem and a tree are the same thing. Students leave here with their eyes restored to them.

Q: Yes, but should the taxpayer –

A: Any taxpayer is welcome to enrol in the course.

Q: Thank you very much, Miss Cole.

A: Do call me Jane.

Now I hear this I'm really amazed at myself. What is it the Coles have which makes one forget anything that would be awkward or inconvenient for them – and makes one say, too, just what they want to hear? I didn't tell Jane Cole about Joe Merton's mad poems! Why not? A sense that Jane Cole has had enough tragedy in her life and doesn't want more? And I never mentioned Gertrud's accusations. Again, one doesn't want to upset Jane Cole No – being in her company is like having one's brain manipulated – gently, carefully, by an outside force.

Just realized it's after 2, and 'the snack lunch is available from 1–2.30' (notice pinned to the board in the hall, halfway between the two landings). I'll go down. But with the catering here I wouldn't be surprised if the small offerings have already gone.

3.00 p.m.

Soup, tepid in a tureen on a mildly warm hotplate, and rolls and Cheddar. Mrs Rees bustling about, in and out of the kitchen. At the refectory table, Paul and Gertrud Ritchie, munching on their rolls. Both looked gloomy – is Gertrud's plan misfiring? No sign of Lana, or of Joe Merton, but Ken was in the kitchen, getting atrociously in Mrs Rees's way. In his drugged state he kept opening the fridge door and peering inside, and sometimes taking out a milk bottle. Mrs Rees shooed him out in the end. I suppose she must be used to some of the 'students' being like that. There's no sign of Ken working on the masterpiece Jason expects, either. There's genius for you!

The weather is turning bad. After the snack I put my head out of the massive door in the front hall and caught the unmistakable whiff of snow. Bright, sparkling Cressley has been replaced by a dull, suffocating monochrome – I think immediately of Muriel's most agonizing poems on claustrophobia and have to fight an urge to get out. What happens if I get snowed in here?

58

Pamela Wright just put her head round my door. Said she had coffee and an electric kettle in her room and would I like a cup. I said I would.

'I always take the kettle with me. Wherever I go. You never know, do you?'

I agreed. We sat in Pamela's room, which is next to mine but as different from it as a hotel room is from a room in the house of a friend – each of us in a small armchair in flowered chintz. The room is completely impersonal. (I have to admit I'm vaguely flattered at having been put in Muriel's room. I have the feeling Jane Cole sums up her guests as they arrive and gives them the room she thinks would suit them.) But then Pamela Wright is very impersonal herself, if one can actually use that word about someone. I can't count how many times I've seen Pamela Wright in my life – in all the shopping streets of the provincial towns in Canada where we used to live when I was a child: going into the chemists', sitting in the teashops, slightly plump, with floury cheeks from using too much powder, and a camel-hair coat and carefully waved grey hair that looks as if it comes with the coat, all part of the same costume. Ken's lucky, to stumble on a motherly soul like Pamela. He might have left school and gone straight into the factory without writing another line of poetry, if it hadn't been for her encouragement.

'How is Ken getting on?' I said. I couldn't refer to the fact I'd eavesdropped right through his interview with Jason Cole and I didn't like to ask if he were in fact a drug addict. Pamela's eyes shone at the question.

'Ken has a real future. Jason Cole saw it at once, I'm glad to say.'

'Oh good.' Another slightly strained silence. I get the feeling Pamela Wright spends a lot of her time alone when she isn't in the company of children. (But she must belong to the W I – and countless other organizations. Perhaps she just feels ill at ease with me.)

'I wonder –' Pamela said at last.

I finished my coffee and put the mug down on the table. (When I say that this conversation took place ten minutes ago and the sky then had come right down almost to the level of the house, I'm amazed at the wild chaos since. Snow isn't falling – it's *attacking*. Hexagonal flakes hurl themselves at the window. With such pandemonium, the snow silence is quite creepy.)

'Did Jane Cole – by any chance – give you the manuscript of Muriel Cole's newly discovered novel?' Pamela Wright took our mugs over to the wash-basin as she spoke, and rinsed them out. 'Because I'd simply *love* to see it! I'm something of an amateur detective, you know! I read about it in the *Guardian* and I did find it so fascinating. It must have been a latish work, I think. And I once bought, at auction, a D. H. Lawrence short story! It was a long time ago, of course. Heaven knows what they fetch now.'

I said of course she could look at the manuscript.

'Don't bother to fetch it. I'll just pop into your room and have a look –'

I told her it was on the table, next to my typewriter. I have a suspicion Pamela Wright heard Jane Cole telling me I was in Muriel's room and she couldn't resist having a quick look – who could? Then I heard her turning the pages – something I dread doing because, fascinating though the novel may be, it means that much more work, to read the whole thing before picking an extract.

I wandered to the bookshelf, which goes right up to the cornice. I couldn't help smiling when I saw the books. Are they supplied by Jane Cole as suitable reading for visitors? *Women and Madness* by Thomas Szasz. *The Death Notebooks* by Anne Sexton. *The Art of Muriel Cole: A Symposium*, which I pulled out – American, of course: I'd never seen it before. And inside it – it fell to the ground, the spine already broken by the look of it – a notebook – old, purplish in colour but stained as if water had been poured over it. Some of the pages had been torn out.

This may sound strange, particularly coming from a professional journalist, but as I leafed through the notebook I suffered an extremely strong sensation of invaded privacy, and after a few moments I had to close it again. Maybe it was the combination of Pamela Wright reading Muriel's unpublished novel in the next room, and of myself reading Muriel's notes – for this was what they undoubtedly were – but, for the first time since arriving at Cressley, I actually felt *haunted* by her. Or maybe it was the snow, which gives a sort of intense privacy to things. I felt my cheeks burn. I thought of Jason, and blankets of snow round us . . . I'd better not go on here, in case my diary is discovered, like Muriel's notebook (although there *are* rather important dissimilarities!). It would be like being run over and having dirty underclothes on, one of the things my grandmother dreaded more than apocalypse.

I did have time, though, before conscience overtook me, to copy out Muriel's first note. It was headed '*Suicide, (Pasternak)*'.

> A man who decides to commit suicide puts a full stop to his being, he turns his back on his past, he declares himself a bankrupt, and his memories to be unreal . . . The continuity of his inner life is broken, his personality is at an end.

Most of the book seems to be quotes – it's an old

commonplace-book of hers, I suppose. On the last page, in blue ink instead of the black she used for the quotes, are some figures.

Royalties: $7\frac{1}{2}\% = £66.72$
Further Sales Royalties: $12\frac{1}{2}\% = £40.45$

I don't know why I copied these out. It's interesting, I think, that Muriel Cole the dreamer and poet should have been interested in money, anxiously calculating her royalties.

'How very rewarding to see an original manuscript like that!' Pamela Wright made me jump as she came noiselessly back into her own room from mine.

I concealed the notebook. I get the idea more and more that Pamela Wright's quite a snooper, in her spinsterish way (not an expression my feminist friends on the *Clarion* would like to hear me use) – and that she's determined to get everything she can out of this rare and exciting opportunity to visit Cressley Grange.

4.30 p.m.

Had to get some air! Wellington boots lent by Jane Cole from the front hall, thick scarf, hat and gloves – the only trouble is, my London coat is too thin for this kind of wild weather. By the time I was halfway down the drive I was quite numb with cold – and deaf, too, to the footsteps that chased after me. Then a heavy weight landed on my shoulders, and I nearly fell – I turned to see Jason Cole.

'It's a poncho from the Andes. It gets very cold up there, you know. Pure llama wool.'

'It certainly is heavy,' I said. 'I thought I might be going to sink into a snowdrift and never emerge again.'

'"The chill – the stupor – and the letting go",' Jason said. 'Do you read Emily Dickinson?'

I had to say I didn't. But somehow it didn't matter. Jason and I walked through the park at Cressley as a wonderful dark blue evening came down over the snow beds. I can't remember what we talked about. The house was changed, now the whiteness had blurred the differences in the architecture, and we stood for quite a long while staring at it, I with mixed feelings about Muriel, and wondering whether she had been happy here (and how much I would be happy here!) and Jason, no doubt, with the feeling of awe he described in 'The Revellers'. A mournful noise, horribly appropriate to the mood Jason was effortlessly creating, drew us into the woods above the drive – and there, perched on a gate like an old man in a sheet, was a white peacock! Jason laughed at my fear.

'He's been here a long time, that one. He likes sitting on the gate – it makes him think he's on his throne back in Persia: look at his gold crown waving there in the snow!'

It certainly was extraordinary. The sky was a very deep blue now, and the ghostly figure of the white peacock looked all the more out of place against the background of winter trees. I slithered on the fresh snow, and Jason gripped my arm.

'Did Muriel like the peacocks?' I said. Jason's arm stiffened and then withdrew: I could have cursed myself.

'She introduced them to Cressley.' He gave a short laugh. 'They may have been some relation, I think. They made the same kind of noise, at least.'

I was surprised by the almost vitriolic tone. How could Jason dedicate his work to Muriel so lovingly, and speak of her as a complaining shrew! And how odd, when con-

63

trasted with the literally idolatrous love and reverence her followers had for her. I hardly dared glance up at Jason as we walked down the slope through the wood to the drive. But I did once – and I felt as if another weight, heavier than the Andean poncho, had landed on me. Jason looked – there is no other word for it – black. He could have been a horseman, a clansman, from those distant, blue mountains. His mouth had become thin and small, and was set in a straight line.

Cressley Grange was lit up for the night. From the façade, invisible in the gloom, patches of orange light indicated 'students' at work, and, higher up, the wide windows of Jane Cole's room. I thought I saw a slight movement at the window as we approached – but it might have been a rook flying across the house, for a whole army of them clattered up out of the branches at the sound of our footsteps. (Looking back on this, I don't think Jane Cole was watching us – I think I was irresistibly reminded of Mrs Danvers in *Rebecca*, forever tweaking at the curtains; and Jason Cole wasn't so unlike Maxim de Winter at that moment, walking to his beloved house with words of hatred for his dead wife hanging behind him in the air.)

The jagged atmosphere made me reckless. I felt personally attacked by Jason's comments on Muriel, as an early reader and admirer of hers would (she was such an intensely personal poet).

'I found an old notebook of Muriel's today,' I said. 'And I thought you ought to know in case you need to put it in the collection. It's only a commonplace-book –'

Jason Cole stopped dead, then walked on very fast, so I had to run to catch up with him.

Now the recklessness was increasing. (My father always used to say, 'Mary, Mary, Quite Contrary' when this mood came over me.) I raced after Jason Cole up the drive

– I had such a desire to protect Muriel (dead all these years!) that I had a good mind to get into the house before Jason and hide the notebook, just because he obviously assumed he had a right to it. But I see now that I am as inconsistent as Jason appears to be, in my attitude to Muriel. A short time ago I was hoping that Gertrud's plan to discredit Jason would prove a failure!

We both reached the front door of Cressley at the same time. Jason opened his mouth – presumably to ask me where the book was – then the door swung open, very quickly, as if someone had been standing behind it, waiting.

They had. It was Jane Cole. Yet at the same time, out of the corner of my eye, I saw *something else*. A figure had been standing behind Jane Cole, and its arms were raised. The hands were holding – what? A stick? No, something longer and sharper. It flitted away into the gloom of the inner hall as soon as the door was opened. I could swear – yes, I know it was Joe Merton. Christ! I *must* tell Jane Cole about those poems. He wouldn't really try it, would he? Punish the cousin for Jason's slighting behaviour? Or *did* I see him? What about the black rook I thought was Jane Cole at the window a few moments before? Is something going wrong with my eyes?

5·45 p.m.

Tea was in the refectory, at the long oak table. The atmosphere was tense. Is this what it's always like here? Or does Jason Cole provide it *gratis* with the course he condescends to attend? Maybe this *is* an exceptional occasion – after all, it's not every day, I suppose, that someone turns up and says that they have proved undeniably that Jason's chief poem holds clues which prompted the suicide of his wife! Jason sat at the far end of the table from the Ritchies, and they all seemed plunged in gloom. I don't know quite how I felt: defiant, I think, at the fact I had annoyed Jason Cole and thus, because he probably wouldn't talk to me again over the weekend, had almost certainly wrecked my piece for the *Clarion*. But I don't care. John Carpenter shouldn't have expected an article out of this daft place, anyway.

The only person who appeared to be in a good mood at tea was Jane Cole. Behind a giant floral tea-cosy she positively beamed. On the polished oak, laid out with plates of scones and biscuits (Mrs Rees, if mean-spirited at breakfast and lunch, clearly enjoys baking), was a collection of holiday brochures. Slabs of blue sea, red sun-umbrellas and bright yellow sand shone in the dim light. Jane Cole was playing around with them like pieces in a jigsaw puzzle – from time to time she pushed one in the direction of Pamela Wright, who was sitting on the long bench on her left, and as she did so she let out sighs of pure pleasure.

'Crete. Isn't it too lovely? But, of course, nothing equals Folégandros. That's where we went every summer. The *divine* sea, sapphire blue . . . And that's where we're going when this nasty winter cold has gone. Aren't we, Jason?'

I couldn't help glancing down the bench, although covertly. Jason looked more bad-tempered than before, if possible. It occurred to me that comparing the sea to a sapphire wasn't his idea of poetic metaphor.

'If only we'd been able to start up the colony,' Jane said. Her voice had become tiny and high like a little girl's, but it carried curiously far. I wonder if she trained as an actress. 'This may interest you, Catherine, for your article.'

66

I nodded politely and leaned forward, buttered scone in hand. Jane Cole's topic seemed to have brought an even greater degree of gloom and tension to the table – both Ritchies had their elbows on the table, heads cupped in hands; Jason was blatantly with his back to Jane and the tea-cosy; Pamela Wright looked apprehensive – but this may have been due to Ken, who was huddled up close to her on the bench like an ugly cygnet, eyes half-closed and hands occasionally straying to his empty plate.

'We were going to found a writers' colony. An island of poets.' Jane Cole let a mystical smile appear in the gaps from the piping voice. 'It was going to be such a wonderful life. The sea was Muriel's true element. Well, you might say it's the element of all true poets. We would lie in the sea, talk and think and compose. The ideal life. Ancient Greece.'

An embarrassed silence followed. Jane Cole leaned right out over the tea-cosy, like an Aztec figurehead thrown into a junk shop above an incongruous bundle of English chintz. 'And we're still going to.' She turned to me suddenly, as if she had forgotten I was there. 'This isn't for publication, Catherine. But now we have the funds . . .'

'We are *not* going to live out there.' Jason had half risen to his feet and was pounding the table. (I couldn't help comparing his rage with Richard's; Richard is so petty in comparison: whining.)

'Jason! You said . . .'

At this juncture, Pamela Wright's cup of tea over-turned. It was still hot, and Ken, who was the main recipient, let out a scream of pain. Consternation! Gertrud rushed forward with a paper napkin, all maternal, her hair swinging wildly; Jane pushed back her chair and stood

67

up, both hands on the table like a fishwife; Jason looked bemused, then swung his legs over the top of the bench and strode to the stairs leading to the Martyr's Room. I found myself catching Paul Ritchie's eye. And I could have sworn he winked at me.

I don't know whether Pamela's cup went over because Jason's fist on the table made vibrations – or whether Ken's nervous movements were accountable. But Ken it was who got the blame. Jane Cole shot him a poisonous look, before leaving her position of command. Then she stomped out of the refectory.

So did the others, after that. Except for Paul: on the pretext of clearing away the plates he lingered by the table, and when Mrs Rees – who had a strange expression on her face, half smiling, as if she'd listened to the conversation and had enjoyed every minute of it – was safely stowing plates and cups on a tray, with an accompanying clatter, he sidled along towards me on the bench.

'That was a strange scene,' he said.

'Yes, wasn't it?' I couldn't help feeling rather – well, nervous. Jason might spring down the stairs from the Martyr's Room at any time, and I didn't want to be caught again.

Paul Ritchie wouldn't be stopped, though. 'That's been Jane Cole's dream for twenty-odd years, you see. This island – it's in the Cyclades, very tiny, and a sort of offspring island from the one where Muriel grew up – well, a couple of years before Muriel died, they were all going to go out there and found this colony. There was a grant from America; both Jason and Muriel were considered the most brilliant poets of their generation; it was all set. Then, of course, Muriel died. Jane kept on wanting to go. Although there hasn't been exactly a shortage of money, what with Jason's own income from his poetry and Muriel's estate, Jason prevaricated. One can see his point – why should he want to go to a place that could only remind him of the past? But the other day – so I gather – he gave in to Jane in a moment of weakness. After the offer from the States for the undiscovered novel, perhaps he felt he didn't have a leg to stand on. Anyway, he could always set Jane up with the colony and go there himself from time to time.'

'So just now –'

'Yes. He clearly changed his mind again. Phew!'

Paul Ritchie fell silent and stared moodily down at the table. I could see his face, distorted, in a knife Mrs Rees had forgotten to clear. From the kitchen came the sounds of loud, business-like washing-up.

'What will – would have happened to Cressley if the colony had been started on the island? Would it have closed down?' I was thinking of my ruined *Clarion* piece. Typical Catherine Treger journalism, my enemies would say. She writes on 'Creativity, can it be bought and taught?' and then a few weeks after it comes out, Cressley Grange closes down!

Paul Ritchie must have guessed what I was thinking, because he shook his head hard. 'I know Jason,' he said. 'He means it. He doesn't want to hear the scheme mentioned again. Cressley will continue as it always did.'

'Poor Jane,' I said, without really meaning it. Yet it does seem sad for her, I must say.

'I ...' Paul looked up and stared at me for a moment. Mrs Rees came in behind us, and pointedly removed the knife from the table in front of him. 'I just don't know what Jane will do. I just don't know,' he said.

Mrs Rees (or so it seemed to me from the corner of my

69

already proven unreliable eye) paused at the threshold of the kitchen. Then she went in, from the dim lights of the refectory – and the knife dropped into the washing-up bowl and hit the other knives and spoons.

6.45 p.m.

Well, now I don't know what to think! I have only fifteen minutes to jot down these notes before going to the pub with Jason, so I'll give just the bare outline –

Yes, the pub with Jason!

After Paul had left the refectory, inviting me, incidentally, to come tomorrow morning for a 'glass of Sunday sherry' in the barn where he and Gertrud are sleeping, I crossed the hall and went into the sitting-room. I thought I might find Jane Cole there: possibly, in her upset state, she might divulge more about Muriel and the past for my miserably starved article. (How nasty this looks. But journalists have to work so much faster than novelists or poets. There's no time to sit around having impressions.) The sitting-room was empty. I sat down opposite the portrait of Muriel Cole and gave myself up to staring at it again. By now it's so familiar I feel Muriel must be walking around in the house somewhere and that I'm always bumping into her without realizing. The eyes, large and dark and oval, seem to stare straight into you. Those high, wide cheekbones, which gave her face a Tartar quality, are familiar to the point where I put up my hand to my own thin cheeks and feel for an instant that I might have borrowed Muriel's beautiful, wide head and am able to look at the world with her unique and original mind.

It still seems far from clear why Muriel had to kill herself. Now I'll copy out A. Alvarez's thoughts on the subject of those extremist poets who walked the tightrope over madness and death. Perhaps I can lead in to my article with it?

> I am suggesting, in short, that the best modern artists have in fact done what that Hiroshima survivor thought impossible: out of their private tribulations they have invented a public 'language which can comfort guinea pigs who do not know the cause of their death'.

and

> The real resistance now is to an art which forces its audience to recognize and accept imaginatively, in their nerve-ends, not the facts of life but the facts of death and violence: absurd, random, gratuitous, unjustified, and inescapably part of the society we have created. 'There is only one liberty,' wrote Camus in his *Notebooks*, 'to come to terms with death. After which, everything is possible.'

Was that what Muriel was doing, in the last year of her tormented life? Coming to terms with death, and, having achieved that, going to meet it all the way?

I just don't know the answer to these questions. Alvarez's language itself is quite alien to me, I now realize: it sounds unreal and dramatic, and I can't believe there are many people in this country who feel *anything* in their nerve-ends. Maybe exalted poets and critics do. Does Mrs Rees? Or Pamela Wright, with her calm acceptance of the horrible state her protégé Ken is in? If she were feeling things in her nerve-ends, she'd be a wreck by now.

Another few minutes and I must go and get ready in the bathroom. Thank goodness I brought some make-up down with me!

71

Jason came into the sitting-room as I was staring at the portrait of Muriel. As I'm used to the oblique way in which he and I seem to see each other and meet, I knew instantly that the quiet step behind me was his.

'Like to come out in half an hour and have a drink, Catherine? There's a good pub at Whitecross, halfway to Ludlow.'

'Oh. Yes . . . I'd love to.'

Then he was gone! So he isn't angry with me after all! Or maybe he wants me to hand over Muriel's notebook and he's decided on friendly tactics. But I don't think so somehow. I think he really likes me!

The minute Jason had gone, I was about to make my way up here when the door burst open and Gertrud ran in.

I can honestly say I've never seen anything like Gertrud's transformation. Her eyes were flashing and rolling. Her mouth was open as if she were in the middle of a silent shout. I stepped back – she was coming at quite a speed – but she charged straight on and got me by both arms. We were both moving by now – me backwards and her forwards, like some ludicrous tango – and I ended up pinioned against the stone mantelpiece, directly under the portrait of Muriel.

'I heard!' Gertrud's shout came out at last. My eardrums are still throbbing from it.

'I heard you and Jason together! Well, I tell you now – if you go out with him, I will destroy you – I will destroy both of you!'

'What on earth do you mean?'

Of course, it was only too obvious what poor Gertrud meant. She was literally demented with jealousy. But her thick accent, which grew a good deal thicker as she shouted, and her mad rolling eyes made me feel more like giggling than being frightened. Not that I enjoyed being pinioned against cold stone – but I had the feeling that, unlike the confrontation with Joe Merton, I could get out of the grip if I tried hard enough.

I did. Gertrud panted for a while after I'd shoved her aside. Then she calmed down a little.

'Don't go near that man. He'll destroy you. For your own sake, Catherine.'

'I'm sure I can't be in too terrible danger,' I said, with what I now see must have been an extremely irritating, smug smile.

Poor Gertrud nearly leapt at my throat again. Then she dropped her voice until it reached the very syllables of doom. 'Look above you, Catherine. Yes. The beautiful, ethereal, golden Muriel. Where is she now?'

'Look, Gertrud, I've got to go and get ready . . .'

'Because of the other one. Muriel could never stand for that. She had never been used to that. And why should she, Catherine? She was his wife, wasn't she? Why had she to suffer the other one? That man should be scourged from the face of the earth, I tell you! And now – he asks you to go out with him – like the first time I came here – many years ago, and he asked me – he said, Paul won't mind, he hardly notices you – and we went to dinner. The evil man! He turned me against Paul then! But we went out – in the car –'.

This was getting too much for me. I didn't relish the idea of standing under the portrait of Muriel any longer, either, compared in Gertrud's obsessed mind with the chief victim. I moved away, but gently, in case this brought another fit.

'What other one?' I said, when I was halfway to the door. Gertrud stood in the middle of the room staring at me, as if she couldn't make up her mind whether to eat me or leave me alone.

73

'You mean you didn't know?' Gertrud gave a low laugh – just for effect, I couldn't help feeling. 'Muriel's sister, Katerina! Yes, that's what he did! How could a woman stand that?'

By this time I was at the door. I had a brief feeling of panic when I tried the door handle: for an awful moment I thought Gertrud had locked us in.

'Look.' Gertrud walked towards me, waving a piece of paper. 'Here is the proof that even in her misery – even betrayed, as she was – Muriel allowed Jason to tell her the truth in "The Revellers". Give it to him in the pub – at your bloody candle-lit dinner – and good luck.'

Gertrud burst into tears. It was an awful sound – as if she were choking, face against a pillow, although in fact she just stood there. Instinctively I moved towards her to give comfort. Gertrud backed away.

'Print it in your paper. Tell him I gave it to you. From Gertrud, mit love. Oh God!'

I slipped out into the hall.

'He should be wiped off the face of the earth,' Gertrud shouted behind me.

It must have been Paul Ritchie's face – he was hanging about by the notice-board and obviously eavesdropping – that made me take the wrong staircase up out of the stone-flagged hall. Paul was pale and trembling violently. I now see he was standing at the bottom of 'my' flight of stairs. I saw him first in the mirror that hangs on the wall between the two staircases. He was ghostly. I can't help shuddering when I remember the expression on his face. As I climbed the stairs, I heard him go into the sitting-room. The door closed with a loud click.

It's always unpleasant to think you're going somewhere you know well and then to find yourself in a strange place. I must have become accustomed already to the land-

74

ing off which Pamela and I sleep – the red-and-blue patterned carpet, bumpy walls that have been papered over in a pink-and-white stripe, and the bathroom opposite Pamela's room, all shiny paint and soap-dishes and towels with bunches of violets on them. In some way I must have been finding the efforts at décor – or homeliness, or whatever it is – reassuring; maybe, in a house like Cressley, where there have been so many tragedies and mysteries, and such long ages of people simply living and dying, an up-to-date touch is an essential thing. (Not that Muriel's room has much of this century about it, but the white paint looks fairly recent.)

At any rate, it's pretty awful at the other side of the house, up the other staircase. Straight away the walls seem higher and narrower, the light is dim, almost green, like the light in old institutions, hospitals or prisons, and an overpowering smell of dust lingers on the landings. The doors to the rooms are uniform with battered paint, and on some of them are enamel plaques: relics from grander days at Cressley. 'Major-General Sir John Cranham'. 'Lady Louisa Parton'. These people must have lived here at the turn of the century, before Jason's father bought the house. How odd it is to think of them here – even odder than trying to envisage Elizabethan occupants, or eighteenth-century ladies with powdered hair. In the Great War, when 'Lady Louisa Parton' wandered in the grounds of Cressley, could she have had a moment of insight into the future and seen a beautiful girl, a tragic Greek heroine, in the Welsh hills, who was to come to the place and then haunt it with the horror of her unhappiness? Would Lady Louisa even have been able to understand the poetry, with its insistence on searing sexual honesty and its frank longing for death? It seems very unlikely. (Might use some of this for the article.)

75

Like a fool, I thought I'd go down the landing, turn left, cross the 'bridge' where Jane Cole lives and find my way back to my quarters. But I ought to know Cressley well enough by now to realize I wouldn't be allowed to get away with it as easily as that! Of course . . . I walked on down the landing. Of course . . . it came to an abrupt end. Across the blocked-up end of the passage stood a gigantic walnut wardrobe – in the semi-darkness, like a troll with arms crossed – and to right and left were rooms, one of which had a chipped plaque swinging over the handle. This would mean the room was unoccupied – the rusty chain would snap off if the knob were turned.

I went into the room on the left. At least, I tried the handle very gently. For some reason, I felt the solution to the blocked-off passage was to be found in there: it was like getting lost in the Natural History Museum and going through rooms of fossils to find the elusive passage. After all, there has to be *some* way the inhabitants of Cressley can get from one part of the house to the other without going out of doors first!

The room I poked my head into is clearly the main dormitory for male 'students'. There are about ten incredibly depressing beds – like beds in the worst kind of prep. school – and each has a grey blanket with a red stripe running down the middle. There is no other furniture, and the stench of dust is appalling. (So the Coles don't spend much of the grant on making their students comfortable: if I feel in a malicious mood when I get back to London, I'll put it in the piece!) The windows are dormer windows, and one of them is cracked. Luckily, this meant some of the snow air from outside could come into the room. I think otherwise I might have come over faint at the mixture of sweat and dust.

Joe Merton was lying on the bed under the cracked

window. Particles of snow fell on his chest, which was bare except for patches of reddish hair. He was slightly propped up on a grey pillow, and with one hand he was holding a black notebook. The other held a pencil: he was scribbling furiously, with the notebook held at an angle of ninety degrees over his eyes.

I retreated as quietly as I could. I think he saw me. But his glassy stare was a reminder of his power to concentrate on his work.

I'm glad I saw Joe Merton. Now – if I could ever find my way – I could drop the poems in on Jane Cole, and warn her that Jason had made another enemy there.

However, easier said than done. I went back along the landing a few paces, and was just about to make up my mind to go the whole way back – down to the front hall and up the facing staircase – when I saw that one of the doors on the right had a frosted glass upper part. Landing doors – green baize doors – I thought of the first time I came to England and stayed with my mother's aunt on the south coast. I felt relieved at the thought of getting through this way. Somehow I didn't relish the idea of passing the sitting-room and hearing the ghastly scene that must have been going on between Gertrud and Paul.

I was only partly right about the door, though. Some early resident of Cressley – carried away by too much enthusiasm perhaps at the notion of modernity – had slung a bathroom right across the landing. Yes – there *is* a door leading out of the other side, also half glass, and the light is assisted further by a glass dome, which reaches up into what looks like a lumber room. To get to the further door you have to walk round a giant of an old bath, which even has claw feet! Cressley can no longer hold any surprises for me.

77

So I thought, until I heard myself let out the kind of scream you associate with horror movies and girls in nighties being chased by wolves.

On a throne in the corner by the door, Ken was sitting. I actually . . .

No, it still makes me feel ill to think of this. I'll describe the throne instead. One of those Victorian lavatories, which are all wickerwork and mounted on a pedestal, like the royal chair of some powerful potentate of British rule. Here, industrialists could ponder the railway book, and the sites of gold mines in India; you can almost hear the crinkle of *The Times* as shares are deliberated. The porcelain handle is discreetly hidden in the mahogany surround. How splendid the Victorians considered themselves!

I saw the needle before I saw Ken. It sounds ridiculous. But it was so murky in there that in my hurry to circumvent the bath and reach the door leading to the other side of the house, I didn't see the figure on the throne in the corner . . . until the glint from the needle in the dim light of a frosted lamp drew me to him. He must have been in the middle of fixing. I walked right into him . . . into it . . . it was horrible.

Ken swore and dropped the needle. There was no light in the bathroom and we both hunted on the large slabs of dingy lino – a purplish colour striped with grey. It was like looking for a needle in the sea. But, miraculously, Ken found it, under one of the claw feet – balls of fluff and dust came up as well in his hands.

'Great.' The first word I have heard Ken say. He wasn't at all embarrassed by my presence, I realized. Nor was he writing his master-work for Jason. (I can't help feeling I should go and say something about this to Pamela. But she must know perfectly well what his habits are. It would only appear busybody of me.)

78

I fled. That's about the only word for it. Ken looked so grey in that putrefying bathroom – I don't find drugs acceptable at all. Poor boy; but moral disapproval always comes up and chokes compassion.

The landing I now found myself walking along was as grimy and depressing as the last one, but at least at the far end there was a shimmer of light. A red crystal lamp, Venetian glass – it was outside Jane's room on the 'bridge', I remembered. Thank goodness! There's a quality of the far side of Cressley which is really disturbing. It's dead, and *slumped*, somehow, like half a body that's been shrugged off. I can't help feeling it's where the ghosts of Cressley live – and there must be plenty of those – whispering and weeping – yes, now I've found it in the notebook, and Muriel thought so, too: 'Go as the shifting walls sing/and women appear/grey dresses rustling/hearts bursting, bursting/at the pitchers' weight on the steep stairs.' Jane Cole might be the guardian of this mouth of the other world, with her red light burning night and day.

I reached Jane's door and tapped on it. This time, she took a long time to answer the call. There was the sound of steps, and a drawer being opened and closed, a rustle of papers.

'Yes?' She peered out at me in the gloom.

'I thought you ought to have a look at these.' I rummaged in my bag and pulled out the poems. 'It's Joe Merton. He seems very . . . er . . . unbalanced to me and –'

'Thank you.' Jane Cole reached out a hand for them. She still stood in the doorway and didn't open the door any wider. I saw she had been crying.

'I hear you're going out to have a drink with Jason,' she said after a pause.

Is it such a big event, then? I had a horrible thought that Jane Cole might be weeping with jealousy, like

Gertrud. But I knew it was because her plans were thwarted: she could go to the pub with Jason any time; she would never get to Greece.

I said I was. Jane Cole told me to have a good time. I went back along the bridge and on to the familiar landing. A note pinned to my door – whose writing? It reminds me of someone – informed me that 'Richard called'.

I'll have to wait to call Richard back until after the drink with Jason. I'm late already. And when I tried the bathroom door a moment ago, Pamela was still in there. What can she be doing? I don't want to be spiteful, but whatever Pamela does to her appearance she'll always look the same. She was handsome, probably, when she was young, though. Good eyes, fine nose –

Jason just put his head round the door. I told him I was waiting for Pamela to get out of the bathroom and then I'd come down. He looked slightly displeased. My God, I wouldn't like to be married to that man!

♦ SUNDAY ♦

II.OO a.m.

NOTES ON CREATIVITY
for the *Clarion*

The *locus in quo* of human creativity is always on the
line of intersection between two planes; and in the
highest form of creativity between the Tragic or Absolute, and the Trivial Plane. The scientist discovers the
working of eternal laws in the ephemeral grain of sand,
or in the contractions of a dead frog's leg hanging on a
washing-line. The artist carves out the image of the god
which he saw hidden in a piece of wood. The comedian
discovers that he has known the god from a plum-
tree.

This interlacing of the two planes is found in all
great works of art, and at the origin of all great
discoveries of science. The artist and scientist are con-
demned – or privileged – to walk on the line of intersection as on a tightrope. At his best moments man is
'that great and true amphibium, whose nature is dis-
posed to live, not only like other creatures in divers
elements, but in divided and distinguished worlds'.
(Arthur Koestler, *The Act of Creation*.)

The above means more to me now than when I read it last
week in preparation for the piece. Jason Cole certainly
gives the impression of being an amphibium – a naturally
creative human being living in several worlds at the same

81

time. But whether this gift can be taught to others, or magically imparted in some way – through the waters of the fountain of Castaly, perhaps – seems to me another matter. People who might otherwise not know how to express ideas are doubtless cheered and helped, but the amphibian quality itself – I don't think it can be passed on. Jason Cole's trouble is that he imagines everyone to have the same degree of imagination as himself. All that this store of imagination needs is unblocking. This is patently absurd. Some people just *don't* have it.

We soon got on to this subject, in the pub at Whitecross, which is like a TV producer's dream of an 'unspoilt' pub: dark, rather damp, with a nasty smell coming off the snooker table and crisp packets littering the floor. Jason bought me a whisky and ginger ale, and a pint of bitter for himself. He looked out of place in the squalid surroundings, like a weathered idol brought down from the mountains to be put on show in a jumble sale.

'It's not only true,' he said. 'It happens all the time. And you'll be able to see it this weekend.'

'With Ken, you mean?'

'Yes. The work he'll produce by the end of the course will be an advance on the work he came here with.'

I didn't want to mention the syringe scene in the bathroom, so I said nothing. In my bag, which I was clutching rather desperately on my knees, was Muriel's notebook, which I had removed from Pamela's room while she went next door to look at the manuscript. It hadn't been mentioned yet, and I didn't want to bring up *that* subject either. So I stayed silent. (Perhaps I had hoped Jason had asked me for a drink for me and not for the notebook.) A bunch of old men in filthy jackets stared at me from the bar. I began to feel depressed.

'Catherine!'

Jason's hand came down on my knee. He must have sensed my spirits sinking. All I can remember now is that I felt a conflict of emotions. The words 'the other one' kept flashing across my mind – I wanted to turn and accuse Jason of betraying me with another – just as if I were Muriel instead of myself! It's really confusing, when one comes up against this kind of irrationality inside one-self. And there must be hundreds of thousands of women like me, who identified with Muriel in the deepest way and want either to wreak revenge on Jason or fall in love with him!

'I'm supposed to be interviewing you,' I said. I edged away, but the hand stayed firm.

'What do you want to know?' Jason said. 'You can cut out my heart if you like and take it back to your room to examine it.'

Why the reference to my room? A reminder that he had definitely caught me spying? A suggestion that he would come later in the night and visit me? And I realized I couldn't ask him about Muriel and her desire for suicide. She was my rival now, and to bring up the past would be to kill the future. (No doubt this is Jason's clever way with female journalists!)

I asked Jason Cole about the change in his poetry. At this, his hand *did* move away, and I cursed myself for bringing any subject up at all. Sex and Intellect don't go together, and it's no use pretending they do. I don't know what Richard would say if he read this! The amount of times I've persuaded him that a joining of intellects, equality and friendship was the ideal prescription for people living together. That romantic love was an inven-tion of the forces of oppression, a phoney adjunct of commercialistic society. Now my Mary Wollstonecraft &

83

Godwin position seemed to melt into thin air.

'You became a Christian,' I said when it became clear that Jason was thinking very carefully before saying anything to a journalist.

'I was always a Christian.'

'No . . . no, but I mean . . . your poetry changed so drastically . . .'

Jason suddenly smiled. I felt it was my heart not his that had been cut out and offered up as a sacrifice. It was certainly hard to believe in the remorse, sense of expiation, and shame which he expresses now in his verse.

'You're right. I was only a Christian in the sense that I was baptized as a child. But a Dionysiac nature can only last a certain number of years. In my old age I feel the weight of the sin of the world. Is that enough for you?'

'But you're not old,' I blurted out before I could stop myself.

'I'm not young. As Muriel and I were when we reached our arms up to the sky and pulled down the words that were dancing there, always further and further away, and always just within our grasp.'

I felt a really horrible pang of jealousy at this. So he *is* still in love with her! How could there have been another? The inscription to Muriel in Jason's latest volume of poetry is a real expression of his feelings. His irritation earlier in the wood, when he compared her to the peacock, was just a husbandly irritation – a memory, painful for him, of her agonizing pain in the last year of her life.

'Did Muriel have a very beautiful voice when she read her poems?' I said. I heard the embarrassment and self-consciousness in my own voice and squirmed.

'A beautiful voice?' Jason's eyes opened wide. 'It was terrible at first. But we used the drum . . .'

'The drum?' I had a sudden vision of the drum in Jason's room, under the frowning, primitive masks.

'Yes. Her best lines came that way. And mine. And when she felt more confident in the rhythm, her voice improved. Certainly.'

There didn't seem to be much more to say after that. I felt Jason to be miles away, living on another planet, in the rhythm of a distant drum. The silence must have hung heavy on him, too, because he went abruptly to the bar and came back with double whiskies for both of us. He sipped constrainedly, while the pub slowly filled with the local, rural population: old men with wheezing breath, and plump, middle-aged women in white, lacy cardigans. The room grew slowly warmer.

Then Jason asked me for Muriel's notebook. I knew he was going to, of course, but I felt a sort of dumb anger, as if he suspected me of trying to keep it for myself. 'I've got it here,' I said.

Then an odd thing happened. One of the marginally younger members of the pub community went over to the juke-box and selected a record. On the way back – just as I was opening my bag and pulling out the notebook – the burly farmer tripped over my legs, which were sticking out from under the table. He sprawled. The table overturned, depositing a sticky mess of whisky and stale crisps on the floor. My bag emptied, and the notebook went spinning across the room.

'Watch out!' Jason shouted.

I ran for the notebook with the kind of urgency there had been in his tone. Anyone would have thought it was a hand grenade from the way he yelled after it. And, accordingly, the ladies of Whitecross half rose, clutching their skirts in horror.

I reached the precious book, which had landed up

against the bar counter. As I picked it up, I realized it had fallen apart even more during the unexpected journey: the spine was completely broken now, and the endpapers were coming unstuck.

I still don't know why I acted the way I did when I saw the sheaf of papers tucked into the now unglued end of the notebook. Muriel must have pushed them in there and then stuck it up again, I thought. And – again as if they were somehow my property – I rescued them from an imminent fall into a puddle of beer and slid them into my pocket.

Throughout all this, Jason's view of me was blocked by people bending and putting the table back on its legs again, righting chairs. The juke-box blared loudly. I reached Jason just as the panicked ladies had resumed their seats and a return to the rural lethargy was beginning to establish itself. I handed him the notebook with, I hope, an innocent expression of desire-to-please, such as all women are taught to use with their superiors, men.

Jason took the book without even a word of thanks.

We drove back to Cressley along narrow lanes with banks so high that it was like being in a maze, guided by instinct alone. (Or so it felt with Jason's driving; he must know the lanes so well.)

Darkness . . . a fox ran in front of the headlights . . . there had obviously been more snow, because the banks were so white that not a tuft of grass nor a leaf showed through. And the roads were slippery, thin white snakes that stretched and twisted without a sign of salt or grit that you would find anywhere civilized.

We reached Cressley as the assembled company was getting up from supper. Through the window into the front hall and the open refectory door, first Gertrud's figure and then Pamela Wright's could be seen passing to and fro with plates and cups on the way to the kitchen.

Jason held me back a moment as I put my hand out to the immense oak front door. 'Thank you for this evening,' he said.

I half turned, uncertain of how to react. In one way, I feel Jason is one of the most unpleasant people I've met. In another, he is undoubtedly the most charming.

Jason bent down and gave me a fleeting kiss on the lips. Then he stood back. The moon, a cruelly thin one, was behind his head in the frost night-sky.

'Katerina!' Jason said.

We walked into the house, to Jane's cool greeting, and the inevitable tomato soup followed by cottage pie. I hoped to see Jason again, but –

◆

'You bitch!' Paul Ritchie said. I was halfway from the refectory to the sitting-room, crossing the inner hall with its two confusing staircases. He put his hand on my shoulder, and pushed me up against the notice-board. From the sitting-room came the hum of voices and a smell of Nescafé. Pamela must have brought her precious hoard downstairs and offered it to Jane Cole.

While these trivial thoughts were flashing across my mind, Paul brought his face right up near to mine and began to hiss at me. I remember wondering why I had ever thought him good-looking. Also, whether he could be heard in the sitting-room, and if so, if someone would come to the rescue.

'You came down here to make trouble. I don't know your reasons. I don't want to hear them. Maybe someone hired you –'

I decided Paul Ritchie had gone raving mad. It's clearly an occupational disease at Cressley – but maybe

mental imbalance and creativity have always gone together.

'What on earth do you mean?'

'Bitch!' Paul pressed the point home. 'The poem, the
analysis. You gave it to Jane. You've completely upset her
now – she's far worse than she was earlier. She's at log-
gerheads with Gertrud – you've made a real rift –'

Slowly it began to dawn on me. The poem! I'd given
Gertrud's computer analysis of 'The Revellers' to Jane
instead of giving her Joe Merton's murderous declaration.
After all, they'd both been in my bag. I'd been in a hurry
as I pulled them out. Then, as Paul continued to shove
me up against the notice-board, another thought dawned.
Jane knew about Gertrud's work on 'The Revellers' already! I'd heard Gertrud talking to her about it. 'I'll show
her the proof!' Yes, that was definitely the case. So why
should I be blamed for this unfortunate revelation? 'She –
Jane – knew about it already . . .' I began.

Paul's eyes bulged. 'How dare you – look, Gertrud
was cured of . . . *him*. Now it's all worse again. I'll *kill
him*. And you're implicated in this too –'

The door of the sitting-room opened and Pamela
Wright came out into the hall, heading in my direction.
She was intent on reading the notice-board, no doubt, to
see if there were any announcements for tomorrow. She
stopped, but not before nearly bumping into us: I hadn't
realized she was short-sighted.

I ran. Paul was away from me at the speed of a hare,
back to the sitting-room and a doubtless stunned and hys-
terical Gertrud. I went up 'my' stairs. I must say, I felt
pretty bad.

Midday

Now feeling a little calmer after writing all this down. After all, it's not *my* fault if Gertrud is upset. And Jane *did* know about 'The Revellers' . . . though I suppose it must have looked rather odd, me thrusting it into her hand. But I can soon explain it was a mistake. (Or can I? You don't feel it would be easy to explain things to the Coles: you're either guilty or innocent with them, quite arbitrarily, like vassals at an ancient court.)

Now the snow is coming down in blinding sheets – if you put your head out of the window, the flakes choke eyes and nose, and hair's white in a second.

Bad, forgetting to call Richard back last night. When I tried a few moments ago, the lines were down. Cressley is like a ghost house – going down to the payphone at the back of the inner hall where Paul held me up last night was like walking in a house that's been empty for years. Something about the chill, and the white light. I suppose all the 'students' are working, preparing for Jason's overseeing of their work.

Except for Joe Merton, no doubt. What is *he* doing? I think maybe I was a bit too quick to jump to conclusions from his poem. They do say, after all, that if you can express your feelings about something, it can prevent you from wanting to commit the act. I've never seen why this should be so, but it's what psychoanalysis would have us believe. Joe Merton certainly expressed his feelings! And I don't think he's capable of anything really dangerous. He's too like a second-rate actor, somehow.

Last night was a weird night. I couldn't get to sleep for ages. I heard Pamela come up and go first to the bathroom, and then to her room. She paced around for a long time – she told me earlier that her sciatica acts up when the weather turns to rain or snow, and maybe it helps her to walk on it. I don't know; but the sound was hard to sleep by – a sort of uneven thump.

On the other side, I could hear Jason moving around in his room. I thought once I heard the small door handle on the inter-communicating door into my room turn, but I think I must have dreamed it.

About halfway through the night there was a loud thunderstorm. I woke with a wildly beating heart. You'd have thought the thunder would have cleared away the snow clouds, but it hasn't. It's like a prison today at Cressley Grange.

Must read what's written on the pieces of paper that fell out of Muriel's notebook in the pub. Must also read some of the just-discovered novel, so as at least to be able to refer to it with some semblance of knowledge in the piece.

But I feel strangely demoralized. I don't want to delve further into Muriel's life, which is, of course, just what John Carpenter wants me to do. Poor Muriel! And who was this sister? Perhaps I should try once more with Jane Cole, and see if I can flush something out of her. Poor Muriel!

I wonder what Melanie and Richard are doing, and whether London is snowbound. Melanie has the most terrible clichés about the snow, coming from Australia with them all ready in case any falls. They're to do with her hatred of the home country, and all this bullshit about dreaming of a white Christmas . . .

I feel quite sleepy, although bed was early enough last

night. I wonder how Muriel and Melanie would have got on together! . . .

5.00 p.m.

This has been the strangest day! Morning: snow falling, and my walk down to the lodge to get a breath of air – and what I found there. Lunch: when I returned from the lodge there was a Land Rover parked outside the front door. A group of people had called on the Coles. Leg of lamb at the trestle table. One quite funny, if rather horrible, incident: at the end of lunch, Joe Merton, who hadn't been at the meal, dragged a fir-tree – he said it had blown down in last night's storm – into the refectory and started decking it with coloured loo-paper. He looked completely mad. I have *no intention* of being snowed in here for Christmas with Joe Merton. But the most embarrassing aspect was Jane Cole's reaction. One of the guests, George Pendy (the Liverpool poet), said loudly as Joe staggered out of the room – presumably to stock up on more Andrex – 'He looks like a regular zombie, Jane. Student, fish or fowl?'

Jane Cole frowned the length of the table. Pendy didn't take the hint, though. He turned to Pamela Wright, who was sitting – with Ken, as always – on his right, and said: 'Zombies are just cheap labour, you know. We must congratulate Miss Cole on solving the servant problem. These big draughty houses are hard to run.'

'Two to clear the plates, please,' said Jane Cole, although several eaters still had mouthfuls to go.

'They still practise it in the Caribbean,' Pendy

persisted. 'Take a man. Drug him. Get the death certificate, while the pulse is still arrested, bury him. Dig him
up that night, and he'll do what you say for the rest of his
days!' Pendy laughed, 'One way of solving the Christmas
decorations, Jane!'

There was an uneasy laugh from Paul Ritchie, and
then silence. Jane Cole's sense of humour seems abysmally
lacking. But when Pendy spouted a few lines of his verse,
I admit I found it hard to decide who was the more absurd,
he or Joe Merton, 'the zombie'. Something like this:

> The sinking pump-girl
> soccer boots melting like Newberry fruits
> a skull waggles his tongue
> at the stumbling crowd.

Jane Cole recovered herself after this, and we hurried
over a semolina pudding which looked as if it had been
cooked the day before by Mrs Rees and lengthily warmed
up.

Then the guests drove off before the snow got too bad.
And they were right. They'll be the last visitors, unless
there's a dramatic thaw. We're snowed in now. Telephone
lines are still down.

On my way back from the lodge I found myself in the
barn with Lana. But first – I have a sort of horror, I think,
of committing this to paper and then being found out (but
that's silly) – I must record the morning's happenings at
the lodge.

Mrs Rees wasn't alone. Her husband was in the
kitchen, drying cups with a cloth. He opened the window
and half leaned out as I came up, and I was quite glad to
see him there: even the walk down the drive in the snow
was enough to make one realize the outing wasn't such a
good idea after all. Snow can be frightening when it comes

at such speed into the face. After a few yards, the house was invisible except for a square, grey shadow that seemed to be hanging several feet from the ground. The road lost its boundaries. And the trees behind fences on either side of the drive were flailing and groaning like wild animals fighting to get free.

Mr Rees opened the back door and offered me a cup of tea in the kitchen. I wondered if he was always so friendly with visitors to Cressley Grange.

'We haven't had a winter like this for fourteen years,' Mr Rees said as I drank the too-sweet tea and tried to imagine myself struggling up the drive again.

'It must be almost impossible to get to Hereford,' I said, thinking of the narrow lanes I had travelled along with Jason last night, and the state they had been in with even a mild fall of snow. Mr Rees nodded his head sagely, just as I was beginning to digest the fact that I might not be able to leave Cressley at all.

'I always say it's lucky Miss Cole put in a deep freeze a couple of years back,' Mr Rees added. 'There's supplies there, even if you do get snowed in.'

My heart sank even further, though I suppose I should have been overjoyed to know I wouldn't starve in the duration of my enforced stay at Cressley. What if I offered a substantial sum to Mr Rees now to try and get me to Hereford? Leave my clothes in the house, plead an illness at home, or a summons from the editor? Mr Rees was in a well-disposed mood . . .

Now I wish to God I had followed that rash but sensible plan. Instead, I accepted another cup of tea and asked Mr Rees about his life, as a journalist can never resist doing. After a brief mention of the past, it transpired, however, that what Mr Rees is really interested in is the future.

'We want to go to America,' he said. 'You know, Los Angeles.'

Mrs Rees appeared from the little front room, as if magically conjured up by the name. She had on her Sunday best: I realized it must be up to the guests at Cressley to prepare Sunday lunch, and imagined Jane Cole even more annoyed with me when I failed to put in a hand.

'We know a couple that went there,' Mrs Rees said. 'Their own house, they had. Five hundred pounds a week.'

'And a pool,' said Mr Rees. 'It would be more now. Mind you, they'd been with the Marquess of Bath at Longleat.'

Mrs Rees snorted. 'I don't know what difference that would have made. If it hadn't been for the article and the pictures.'

'Yes,' Mr Rees said, filling my mug again. 'Along with that maid to old Lady Astor. In the *Sunday Telegraph* colour magazine . . .'

I saw what Mr and Mrs Rees wanted. The power of publicity! I felt irritated, and at the same time I needed badly to go to the lavatory – the hot tea, after the cold outside, had viciously attacked my bladder. I rose from the table and asked the way.

Otherwise, I would have gone back up the drive. Life's little ironies: a bursting bladder that alters history in its course.

'On the right at the top of the stairs,' Mrs Rees said in an anxious voice, suggesting her fears that the bathroom might not quite measure up to a colour magazine photograph.

'I was saying we haven't had a winter like this for a good fourteen years,' Mr Rees said, to cover the silence as I edged my way past him in the tiny kitchen. Mrs Rees

94

snorted again. As with many couples, constant contradiction seems to be the rhythm of their life.

'Fourteen years! It's twenty-one years, more like! The last big snows was when Mrs Cole went. You're not telling me you've forgotten that!'

I reached the kitchen door, outside which climbed a narrow staircase to the upper floor. The Reeses must have noticed me pause at the mention of Muriel, and I thought Mr Rees gave me a sly look before concurring with his wife.

As if to expunge himself of any guilt at his behaviour, Mr Rees thrust his hands into the washing-up water again. He then dried them vigorously and leaned over to take my right hand with his left, like a child entering into a game of ring-a-roses. 'Time flies, that's what it is. Twenty-one years ago it surely is. And they had to pull the hearse out of the snow on the road to Ludlow.' He pulled his hand free and crossed himself, and Mrs Rees followed suit – there was suddenly a very Irish-Catholic feeling in that kitchen. 'That was a day and a half,' he ended with a sigh.

I went up the stairs, but before I got to the top I understood the game. I give the Reeses an *Upstairs, Downstairs* glamorous coverage, enabling them to receive offers from movie moguls, and they give me details, perhaps never before revealed, of Muriel's death and her last months at Cressley Grange. I'd met their sort before –indeed, the other sort, the 'gems' of a staid English past, have by now become almost extinct.

As it happened, I didn't need to consider the deal. (And luckily: it's very improbable that the editor of the *Clarion* magazine, a dour man with a firm eye on advertising revenue, would have thought anything newsworthy in the Reeses and their life of service to a poet who was probably of no interest to him.)

A moaning sound was coming from the other side of the bathroom wall. The lodge has only two bedrooms, one either side of the bathroom, and I'd already glimpsed the Reeses', all magenta satin pillows and pictures in oil of the Welsh hills. This must be the spare room – but they hadn't alluded to having a guest in the house.

Several rather unpleasant thoughts went through my mind, of the Glamis Monster variety. Then I pulled myself together. Why should they mention a visitor? It just seemed odd that someone so clearly in pain should be left untended in the upstairs room.

The door wasn't closed properly, and I pushed it open and went in.

An old woman was lying in a narrow bed, in a frugally furnished room. She was propped up on the pillows and it was possible to see, even from the doorway, that she was more in a state of frustration at not being allowed to get up than in a condition of mental derangement.

She saw me in the shadows by the door (her bed was under the window, and in the glare from the snow she could more easily see me than I her. But I saw that her skin was sallow and wrinkled and white hair stood out in puffs from a partially balding scalp. She seemed an unlikely adjunct to Mrs Rees's life). Then she leaned forward and spoke.

'Katerina!' the old woman said.

I went up closer to the bed. My heart was thumping again, and I had a feeling of acute embarrassment, as if I had been caught out somehow – but for what, I don't know.

'Who are you?' I tried to sound conversational; I wondered if Mrs Rees could hear us in the kitchen.

'Katerina – and I thought you were there!' There were tears in the old woman's eyes. 'I never thought to see you again. They told me you were really gone. But here you are – well, Katerina, I can hardly believe it!'

Something quite unpleasant happened to me at that point. My throat became unbearably dry and at the same time a burning heat spread over my face. I was unable to move – either towards the old woman or away from her, to the door. And the worst of it was that I still knew the old woman was perfectly sane – she was simply under the impression she was seeing a ghost.

For a time, ghost that I was, I couldn't even get out the questions which had steered me through life, disconcerting others before I could be disconcerted myself. I gaped, an apparition that had gone red in the face. The old woman was still staring up at me – and I'm not sure she didn't mutter, 'You're just as pretty as I knew you were, Katerina,' or something like it, before I managed to come to my senses. It was the sudden knowledge that jolted me: the sound of Jason's voice as he said the name; the old woman's avid, familiar tone.

'Where is Katerina now?' I heard myself ask.

The old woman gave a surprising laugh, low and knowing, as if she had often thought about precisely that.

'She's meant to have gone back to Greece, dear. But you know as well as I do where she really is. My dear, I thank you for coming to see me. Because – at last – I can tell you what really happened . . .'

A door slammed under us; Mrs Rees's voice rang up the stairs.

'Auntie! Is that young lady out of the bathroom yet?'

There was suspicion in the voice. It freed me from my paralysed stance, and I went on tiptoe to the bed, fast.

97

'Where is she?' I hissed into the poor old woman's ear. 'I have to know. I mean it.'

'My dear, my dear.' At such close quarters, it was becoming increasingly clear that the old woman was in a good deal of pain. A shadow crossed her face as she shifted her leg under the blankets. 'Where did they put the corpse, dear?'

'What corpse?'

I was as astonished by the old woman's answer as if she had announced her recent arrival from outer space. Mrs Rees was now panting up the stairs, and I was too taken aback to go any further. But the old woman succeeded in amazing me once more – just as Mrs Rees's plump hand turned the doorknob and a portion of chunky tweed skirt and leg shot into the room.

'Frozen dead for a millennium,' the old woman said. She then closed her eyes and lay back on the uncomfortable, spare-room pillows.

◆

As I write this, I realize my time is running out before the Sunday evening meeting at 7 p.m. when work undertaken at the course will be read and commented on by Jason Cole, prior to 'rewriting' tomorrow and Tuesday – and I must be there, to report on the way a great poet turns editor: and on Government funds, spending of.

But first, it is essential to record what I saw with my own eyes. (That's a funny way to put it, who else's eyes might I have, or am I already partly convinced I'm a reincarnation of Muriel's sister, Katerina?) And that is that Mrs Rees is embarrassed by her aunt, who is 'down from the North' on a visit for the first time in – yes – twenty-one years. She, Mrs Rees, is afraid her aunt will spill some very well-concealed beans. Well, she already has.

When I left the lodge, and with less ceremony than I had received earlier, I started up the drive in blinding snow, which was at least at my back this time, giving me clearer visibility than before. If it hadn't been for that, I would never have seen the old woman in the trees, on the land that slopes up away from the drive, on the north side. How had she got out so quickly, and in this weather? She was hobbling along – she was carrying a stick and prodding the ground with it – and every now and then she came to a halt and scrabbled away at the ground like a terrier. She had on a black coat and a red scarf. I'll never forget –

I went up through the trees, dodging behind them so as not to be seen. I came within about four feet of her. We were on high ground –

The old woman had made a fairly deep hole in the snow. She plunged in her hand and started pulling out dead beech leaves, which made a rusty gash on the white hillside.

Hillside! I knew it was the burial mound. That was where Jason had taken me where the white peacock had stood flapping on the broken gate. I knew suddenly, too, with a cold feeling far worse than the freezing cold of a December afternoon in fading light and frost rising, what the old woman was searching for in that absurd, childish hole. My feet, in flimsy boots, sank into a drift and stayed there.

How could she have known the exact spot? But of course she *would* know, if she had seen it. Twenty-one years ago. She would know the tree, the position –

Mrs Rees's aunt scrabbled a bit longer. Then she tugged hard, and something came out. I can't say it was a – a part of someone – but I know it wasn't a stick. It was getting dark fast – snowflakes were dancing between the old woman and me; in a blue evening sky the thin moon made its appearance again but gave no light. I know it wasn't a stick –

I didn't wait to see what the old woman did next. I ran.

To the barn: had to go there because after my flight up the drive the front door was locked – as in a nightmare!

No sign of Paul or Gertrud, although the light was on in their room.

Lana was at home, though – and I realized I'd almost decided she must have vanished from Cressley, she's been so invisible lately.

Inside the room where Lana sleeps: blue, blue everywhere. Sea painted on the walls, complete with spray and flying dolphins. Must be Jane Cole's fantasy room, where she dreams of Greece. There are even sea anemones, lovingly painted in a frieze on the walls, and a marble ruin sticking out from a green headland. Clumsy, amateurish stuff. Upsetting, somehow. But then I was upset anyway.

Lana tells me I'm quite wrong to imagine that this is Jane Cole's décor. She faces me, pale and white but still sticking to her ground – as Muriel's true champion, the avenging angel.

LANA: This was where Muriel slept in her last year here. I'm so happy to be in this room.
SELF *awkwardly*: But I'm in Muriel's room – in the main house. Jane Cole said so.
LANA *fiercely*: She's lying! Truly, Catherine, haven't you noticed how much lying is going on?
SELF: Well, I –
LANA: Why don't the Coles want anyone to know Muriel

was here? Look, here's the proof of it. I found it. Under the carpet. Here.

Lana had been picking at the carpet, by the bed, she said (and she's just the nervous type: there were signs on the blue walls, too, of her fingernails picking away and plaster showing through), and she'd come upon a tiled floor underneath. There was such a pretty design – flowers and fish and quite old-looking – that she'd decided to cut the carpet away a few inches and then sew it back in before Jane Cole noticed anything. (These neurotics!) Then she'd seen it. And there it was.

The letters were crudely carved. M U. That was all.

SELF: How do you know she was here in her last year, Lana, from this?

LANA: She painted the walls in 1967. Look, it says down here: 1967. And she must have tried to carve her name from the bed, when she was in pain. It's just about as far as you can reach with a penknife.

For some reason I shuddered. Lana must have noticed, because she gave me the first real smile since she arrived.

'She wanted us all to know,' she said. 'Muriel was banished from the house, from her husband. She died alone, and in pain. You should publish these discoveries, Catherine.'

But there are more discoveries than Lana knows of. After extracting a promise that she would turn up for the 7 p.m. meeting with her work – 'It's all dictated by her,' she said, 'I don't think he'll like me to read it out –' I went in the back door and reached my room, thank God, without bumping into anyone.

Lana doesn't know about Muriel's sister Katerina. She

mustn't know. Does it seem now that Muriel's *sister* was sleeping in this room where I sit, and not Muriel herself? Muriel, relegated to the barn . . .

6.45 p.m.

Jane has just put her head round the door. Says the phone is mended! And a thaw forecast – I shall be able to get home after all! Hooray!

Decision: Leave these mysteries of Muriel to another generation of Cole-cultists. Do best with article and forget the whole set-up.

Next door I can hear Pamela getting ready for the session downstairs – I'd better run. But I can't help looking at a page that fell out of Muriel's notebook.

On it, there are eight lines:

> And I
> roll-shut your sister eyes.
> The pupils heave,
> go up, without a string.
>
> I am Medea,
> the one who rode
> and hunted you in the white
> streets, the abacus of death.

What are these lines telling me? Can they really be by Muriel Cole? Muriel the sufferer, the hard-done-by, as Mrs Rees vindictively described her? These aggressive, almost murderous –

Jane's gong in the hall sounds for the second time. Where can I put these notes? Down my tights, like at school!

◆ MONDAY ◆

7.30 a.m.

Don't think I've ever felt quite like this in my life. I shouldn't have done it. Traitor.

But traitor to whom? Richard wouldn't care. Lost in his job, dreaming of the strong-limbed girl in Australia who had the nerve to turn him down ten years ago.

To the *Clarion*? But it's practically a hallowed tradition that women journalists sleep with the famous men they interview. There's giggling afterwards, and significant looks, and the whisper, 'If only I could say what I really know . . .' And maybe that's what I find revolting about the whole thing: it's not hallowed, it's hackneyed. I don't want to feel about Jason that way.

To Muriel? She's been dead and gone a long time. No, the eerie thing, now I look at it closely, is it's like betraying Katerina, the second self, or the previous reincarnation, or the look-alike, or whatever I am to her.

Perhaps because Jason came into this room, which I'm more and more convinced had been hers, at any rate in the last year of Muriel's life, and not Muriel's . . . did I dream he called me by that name? Katerina?

I kept wondering if we were waking Pamela; it's awful how these trivial thoughts can come in at such times! I did hear Pamela next door, though, as Jason and I lay quietly afterwards – I'm sure I did. Is she the kind of person, I wonder, to be shocked by casual sex? It must be so alien to her experience and way of life . . . I feel sorry if we embarrassed her.

Now it's over, and it's early in the morning, and I must take stock of myself. Outside, the sky is a bright pale blue. The thaw never came. Snow did instead, and we are truly snowed in, only this time in an insouciant Christmas-card landscape, instead of the oppressive gloom of yesterday. I bet the phone is down again. I hardly care. I didn't take advantage of it working to call Richard last night, and if I'd really wanted to, I would have.

There was the sound of thunder in the night again, too, after Jason had gone from my bed and through the communicating door into his room. These storms seem to be part of the Cole mystique – at tea yesterday Jane was boasting about the thunder the night before, saying it was louder and more magnificent over the hills at Cressley than anywhere else in the area. Something Byronic for her to get her teeth into, I suppose.

I'm putting off making a decision about the future. All the symptoms of Catherine Treger absence of re-solve are there: bursts of enthusiasm to stay at Cressley for the rest of my days, humbly serving the Coles and their creative writing courses (as opposed to writing an acerbic article about them); the desire to walk, if neces-sary, through snow-drifts all thirty-eight miles to Here-ford station rather than stay a moment longer in the pres-ence of Jason; an unpleasant self-serving wish to 'make everything all right' with anyone in the house who might be offended or jealous if they knew what had taken place between Jason and myself. At present I don't feel I can do any of them.

Gertrud is the person I would have to go and see before leaving. Last night, after we had all collected in the sitting-room and were waiting for the royal presence of

Jason, she came and stood very obviously near me, and I had to pretend to smile in a friendly way into her brown eyes glittering with envy, and her mouth, which had taken on a horrible boat-shaped curve, like the mouth of a witch drawn in a fairy-tale book. She began to speak at once, and I was uncomfortably aware of derisive glances from Joe Merton and Ken at the sight of us together – though why I should care what *they* think, God only knows. Paul was staring at us too, but in a different way, as if he was frightened Gertrud might go off the deep end altogether.

'So how did your drink in the pub go?' was the predictable question, hissed loudly so Jane Cole and Pamela, who were standing under the portrait of Muriel, looked up and then down again, ill at ease.

I told Gertrud it had 'gone' all right. But I'm sure she must have fore-sensed, in the way women do, what was going to happen between Jason and me later that night, because she grabbed my arm and drew me even closer. Jane Cole gave a quick glance and started forward – so did Paul – but Gertrud was quicker than that, and she had me following her bony wrist to the far end of the room, where the piano stood. 'There's something you ought to know.' She breathed up into my face. 'Outside. By the drive. Didn't you see?'

Jason came into the room. I felt him look down the far end at Gertrud and me, and my cheeks burned: Gertrud was bad news to be with, and I hated to give the impression that she and I were ganging up, thus ruining prospects with Jason later. But at the same time her words couldn't be blocked out – I saw the figure of Mrs Rees's aunt, and the night sky coming down over the burial mound.

'There's one waiting for you,' Gertrud said, and

giggled. 'A nice quiet grave waiting for you out there, Miss Catherine Clarion.'

I don't know why, but instead of privately certifying Gertrud for these mad remarks, I found myself instantly in a state of confusion – one of those states of geographical confusion that completely preoccupy the mind until the locus of what the brain is trying to find has been fixed upon. I was walking up the drive with Jason ... the house was just ahead of us and we stumbled off into the woods on the right, on dark ground, up a steep incline. The *burial mound* ... and yet, coming up from the lodge in the morning, after visiting Mr and Mrs Rees, I had seen the old woman on the north of the drive amongst the trees, on what I had thought was the same mound ...

'There are two graves out there, Catherine,' Gertrud said. 'One's in an artificial hill, down by the lodge, that's the one waiting for you. It's like a rubbish tip, really. The other is where Muriel is buried – but no one knows, or the mad American feminist tourists would try to dig her up. They say she's in Ludlow churchyard. No. She's out there.'

My mind had accommodated the two sites, and as it recovered from the shock I began to realize that Gertrud was indeed completely insane. But it's hard, sometimes, when information comes to you like that, at the same time as a strong visual memory, not to fall into instant credulity.

Jason announced that we would start with Lana reading her work. Jane signalled to Gertrud to come out of the shadows at the far end of the room, and I followed her.

But I was hardly aware of the droning voice, the Muriel-derived syllables, that spilled out into the room.

Why were there two burial mounds out there? Which one had Mrs Rees's aunt been searching in so desperately? Was Muriel buried in one and Katerina her sister in the other? Why had there never been any mention of the sister? Or the scandal, which there had obviously been?

I only snapped to attention when the hypnotic sound of Lana's voice stopped suddenly, at a barked order from Jane Cole. What had happened? Paul Ritchie, who was sitting on the sofa with Gertrud on one side and me on the other – to keep us apart and prevent further salacious details being spilt to the press, no doubt – turned to me, frowning when I showed surprise.

'This has happened before,' he said. 'A few years ago. The girl should never have been allowed in here.'

Without begging Lana, who was perched on a hard-backed chair under Muriel's portrait, trembling but defiant, to give me a repeat performance, I could guess what had taken place. Lana had read a poem of vengeance, of reprisal for her heroine's death. Jason just sat there – like a savage god himself, I couldn't help thinking – and stared straight ahead. And I had to repress a twinge of fear. What about Joe Merton? It certainly seems the Coles are going to get a heavy time of it this week!

Note here for article: When is a work of art removed from the work-of-art category by virtue of the sentiments it expresses? If, for instance, Lana's poem had been a master-piece (which I very much doubt!), then would the fact it gave vent to murderous feelings and cruel aspersions invalidate it? I can't see that this would be so – and the same would be true of Joe Merton's efforts, evidently, if he were able to produce a work of art. Thus a true work of art is infinitely more dangerous than an amateurish botch. Jane Cole shouldn't have bothered to stop Lana in her tracks!

Luckily, anyway, there was no question of hearing Joe

Merton's tussles with the muse. No sooner had Lana, shivering by now as if the snow outside had come right into the room, been escorted to the barn by a kindly and concerned Paul Ritchie (poor Lana, I hope she's all right), than a great hullabaloo started up in the hall between the sitting-room and the refectory. Jason was the first to run to the door. Pamela Wright leapt from her seat and followed hot on his heels. Of course: she had recognized the voice of her protégé, her beloved Ken.

I must say, I wouldn't even have recognized the voice as human. It was a scream – like the kind of scream you hear from the zoo at night, when you can't imagine which species of animal is venting its despair and fury, and a vision of panthers and pumas and elephants and lions goes across your mind's eye in a nightmare parade. The kind of scream that turns the night inside out, and makes you long for day. (Would keep this for article except I don't think the *Clarion* is going to want me to publish news of heroin addicts on creative writing courses that are being supported by government grants).

Ken has lost his syringe! When the sitting-room door was opened, and Jason and Pamela reached him, Ken was howling on hands and knees on the strip of Persian carpet under the table and the notice-board. He yelled out what he was looking for without any interrogation.

Again, I can't help smiling as I record all this. The person most shocked by Ken's junkie collapse, surprisingly, was Jane Cole – you'd have thought she had been through enough dramatic scenes in the past to inure her for ever. Gertrud simply looked sulky, as if Jason's attentions to others, whoever they are, send her into this sullen state without fail. Paul, who arrived back from the barn just too late to catch the zoo noises, bustled about, picking up Ken's legs while Pamela seemed to be trying to hold him down by the head. Then Jason and Paul carried Ken up the stairs to the dormitory.

I wouldn't have wanted to share a room with Ken in that condition, but Joe Merton looked quite oblivious. He was so stunned, I think, at the news that the readings had been cancelled for the evening, and therefore that his own shriek of fury and spite would have to go unuttered, that the effects of a night with Ken going cold turkey never crossed his mind.

At any rate, the failure of the evening made it possible for Jason and me to go out, sliding in his car down muddy lanes which gave every appearance of thaw. (They must be impassable now.) There's a restaurant, a draughty converted granary, in the same village as the pub we visited. I can't remember much about it. Prim, middle-class couple serving up scallop terrine and kiwi fruit in French Provençal dishes, piped music, whistling cold winds round the ankles. A large dog, which kept sniffing at my tights, as if it could tell my notes were bulging in them at the top and its idea of sport was to retrieve them.

What I do know is I'll feel perpetually ashamed of myself for failing, with Jason, to ask more of the Muriel-and-Katerina mystery. I could have gleaned *something*, I'm sure of that.

But, of course, I didn't ... After a bottle of wine, and two brandies each, we lurched home on roads already stiffening white with frost at the edges. Jason's arm was round me, and I remember I kept twisting and craning to stare out of the window at the new moon, which seemed to hold some special significance for us ...

Vanity, thy name is woman ...

8.45 a.m.

Feeling more sober now.

Resolution: Take advantage of a quiet day here to write up notes. Can't get out anyway – the snow outside lies there like a saucer, tempting, filled with white milk. (Am I getting poetic? It must be the atmosphere of Cressley, seeping through at last!)

Warning: Don't let Jason go to your head. Jobs aren't so easily come by nowadays, and to write a bad piece about this place might result in John Carpenter deciding to send someone else to that science fiction conference in Mexico in the spring. These little adventures are nothing to Jason – or to me, for that matter – despite the beautiful things he said.

Say to yourself: Think of the number of times you've done this sort of thing. It's practically a classified ad: 'Liberated attractive journalist, early 30s, will screw anyone sufficiently interesting and likely to advance career, no strings attached.' Yet somehow, it seems all wrong here . . .

MURIEL

Start of piece. 'Muriel Cole was the light and inspiration of the women's movement. From the first excited consciousness-raising groups of the mid-Sixties, to the rape-conscious, "post-feminist" Eighties, Muriel Cole has been a beacon – more of a totem is perhaps the correct way of putting it – of women's pain, struggle and sacrifice.

Her particular pain, in a life which culminated in morphine addiction and suicide, was the pain of the masochist, of the woman who invites suffering because society has brought her up to expect it. Her unhappiness in her marriage, her physical suffering after the car accident and the sense of great deprivation and inadequacy after the miscarriage of her child, combined with feelings of inferiority as a poet, despite her great gifts, led her to the only way out: self-obliteration. But at Cressley Grange last week I stumbled on a possible "other" Muriel Cole . . .'

♦

No. I can't say that. I don't have the evidence for the existence of Katerina. And I have only the fragment of the poem. What would it mean, unless – well, it's horrible to say – the body of Katerina were actually to be found in the grounds here? What good would it do if the body *were* found? Muriel dead, would they interrogate Jason at length? How he would suffer – there's that word again.

And what real proof do I have that Gertrud is right, for all her talk of 'analysis', and Jason isn't just playing games in his most famous poem? I can see John Carpenter's face when I blithely present a piece like that! All the schools in England would have to change the curriculum! And if Muriel turned out not to be the Muriel we've all been brought up to believe in . . .

There's a jinx on this article. I can't write it. I should maybe talk to Jane Cole again, but she's more likely to give information to the entrails of a chicken than to me. The brightness of the snow outside is beginning to make me feel sleepy. It's a white world, innocent with snow, you can hardly see the artificial hills of the dead from here. It's slightly sickening, too: the sun on the snow makes it shine like that sugar that comes in crystals and

leaves too strong a taste. I feel I could just lie down in it –
remembering the lines Jason quoted on our first walk,
from Emily Dickinson: 'the chill – the stupor – and the
letting go . . .'

10.00 a.m.

It's awful. I can't believe it.

Jason is dead.

He was found half an hour ago when he hadn't gone
downstairs for breakfast.

Oh God.

Midday

Jason was found dead in bed. There were 'possible signs
of a struggle'. Jane found him, going in with tea . . . who,
who could have wanted to murder this wonderful man?
His vitality, his greatness . . . what am I saying? I can't
bear it. I can't believe it.

1.00 p.m.

We've all been in the sitting-room, some sitting, some
pacing, while Mrs Rees cooks a risotto and the smells
come in under the door. She's right I'm sure, as hysteria
would erupt without food, but I don't think I've ever
been so nauseated by the smell of cooking. The lines

are down – of course – the snow hard and adamant – so the undertakers and the police and whatever can't get here.

Gertrud was the calmest, surprisingly. She stood by the window that looks out on to the courtyard and the barn, and kept saying 'Poor girl!' in a low, compassionate voice. She's certain Lana killed Jason. But I don't feel ready yet to place blame on anyone . . . Jason is dead. That's the terrible thing.

I went to see him, although I'm sure Jane Cole would have forbidden it. Apart from his murderer, I was the last person to see him alive. I had to see him once more. His face was stern and sad, as if he had gone on the punishing journey foreseen in his later poems and had found it as hard and joyless as he expected. He looked extremely familiar, as if I had known him all my life: his was no death of a stranger. The sheets were pulled up under his chin. The 'signs of struggle' described by Jane Cole had been left for the police to investigate, and they were less than I'd imagined – a chair by the bed overturned, the chest of drawers half pulled out into the room, as if someone had tried to hide behind it, an African mask fallen on to the drum below.

Who could it have been –

I don't want to think yet. I touched his cold neck under the sheet and tiptoed back into my room as if I'd been thieving. But I did take something: Jason's image, as indelibly stamped in my mind as a wax death-mask. No one will ever be able to take it away from me.

2.30 p.m.

That was the most terrible lunch I ever sat through. There was complete silence at the table. Paul and Gertrud sat together, at the far end of the trestle table, like wounded birds on a perch. It was wrong, somehow, to see Paul in Jason's place, which he had taken, I suppose, quite unconsciously. Jane, at the head – I've never seen a face *set* like that, and aged too: the lines from nose to chin deeply engraved and lips clamped as if they would never open again. Joe Merton wolfing his food as if he's never eaten before. Lana staring at him in disgust – eating nothing. And Ken and Pamela halfway along the trestle bench: Ken sheet-white, Pamela with a hand on his knee. Mrs Rees circled the table with a salad and Heinz mayonnaise. She must have known no one would get up and help themselves. What did her face say? It was impossible to tell. Like a nurse, working on a terminal case . . .

Except Jason is dead already.

You could feel the suspicion at the table.

I must take hold of myself. Here, in the shadow of Muriel, horrible and depressing and grotesque thoughts come to mind too easily. The language of pure hopelessness. But she knew more of death than I do. She could handle it . . . I can't.

The cloud of suspicion lies on Ken. Jane announced at the end of lunch that a syringe had been found in the passage outside Jason's room. She pulled it out of her bag. It was the first sentence she uttered. Terrifying! It was Ken's syringe all right – you should have seen him

114

look away from it. Paul and Gertrud cowered at their end of the table as if a gun had been whipped from out of Jane's bag.

Of course, Paul and Gertrud would have a particular hatred and fear of syringes. Muriel's addiction – Gertrud told me they were with her often in the last year of her life.

The snow outside is as unmovable as ever. We can't be sealed up here with dead Jason . . . it's just not possible. But it is.

I'd give everything in the world to talk to Richard in London now. How can they mend the phone when the snow's as bad as this?

Why should Ken kill Jason? Because Jason had taken his syringe, perhaps, in an effort to cure him? Had confiscated it, like a schoolmaster? If Ken was the most promising talent Jason had come across for a long time, it was unbearable to him, conceivably, that Ken was on the road to killing himself with drugs . . .

Yes, it's possible. Jason was on such close terms with death, he could see it coming, he was trying to save Ken's life. And for his pains, Ken killed him.

3.45 p.m.

That sleep was necessary. It's almost dark now outside, and when I woke, before I remembered what happened, I felt so strangely happy. I think I took the dark for a great flood, which would crack the porcelain snow and release me from this valley of death. I lay there quite snugly . . .

This is too much. The electricity has gone now. A candle in a green-and-white china holder, and only one of them, is all I have to write by. I must keep writing. If I tried to go out, I'd sink like a traveller in a freezing waste. If I go downstairs, I'll come up against those faces . . .

Try and remember. Try and remember. Jason and I. Coming back from dinner in the restaurant. Who was still up and about at Cressley Grange?

Paul I remember, he gave us a strange smile when we came in, rather uncertain on our feet. He went off to the barn. No sign of Gertrud . . .

The fact is, anyone could have murdered Jason after he left my bed.

I have to face up to the fact that nearly everyone here could have wanted to. It's a terrible thing to say, but Jane, in her desperate desire for Greece, and because of his cruel, taunting way of treating her hopes and longings, could have reached the end of her tether and gone to kill him in the depths of the night.

Joe Merton – well, he practically announced he was going to. Why didn't I take the threat more seriously? I still have the bloody poem in my bag, for God's sake . . . I could be responsible for the death of Jason Cole, through my own irresponsibility . . . and when I gave the wrong poem to Jane, I didn't even rectify the situation later . . .

Pamela Wright, in protection of Ken. After all, I did hear movements from her room very late, after Jason had left me. Suppose she sensed that Ken was on the prowl in this part of the house, and went to see what he was doing? Suppose, even, she *knew* Jason had confiscated the syringe, had seen him do it. And perhaps she saw Ken surprised by Jason, as he crept into his room, Jason overcoming Ken easily . . . there had been a struggle . . .

But was Jason really killed with a syringe?

In the silence at lunch, no mention of the weapon. We

are expected to take Jane Cole's word for it: Jason has been murdered. There was a struggle. And yet, when I went to see him, his face and head were untouched. Did Ken inject him with a lethal dose of heroin? How could he? Jason was a very strong man. No, that's not the way it happened . . .

First, find out how it was done. Yet I dread going downstairs . . . especially now it's dark. Lana. Oh, if anyone ever wanted to murder, it's that girl Lana. I think of her standing in the amateurishly painted room in the barn, and drawing back the carpet she'd pulled at with her nail-bitten fingers, and showing me triumphantly: MU. Suppose she was right, and twenty-one years ago there was another murder mystery at Cressley Grange . . .

Not a suicide. A murder. MU for Muriel. MU for murder, too.

Let these thoughts out. They're better expressed than kept in. It's twenty-one years ago to the day that Muriel died. This is a murder of revenge . . .

Gertrud. Despised, rejected. Going to his room when she couldn't bear her sleepless night any longer, and Paul Ritchie beside her instead of *him* . . . jealous perhaps, of me (I have to stand up to this), anxious to find us together. Voyeurism, despair, jealousy. She goes to his room, shows him her findings on 'The Revellers'. She says she will pay Jason for the misery he has given women – Muriel, herself, Katerina – she attacks him and there's a struggle . . . she fires at him . . .

There must be a pistol shot on Jason's body, under the sheet.

I didn't hear it. Because of the thunder. Of course, how convenient for Gertrud –

Or for Paul, who may be of stronger stuff than at first appears. Small, dark, burning eyes. His horror that

117

Gertrud is still as obsessedly in love with Jason as she ever was. His future with Jason in jeopardy, and therefore his career, for how can Jason continue to help him if Gertrud has returned to a state bordering on the psychotic? Rage, impatience with the years wasted trying to wean Gertrud from her futile love for Jason Cole? . . .

I could go now, although I have only this candle, and find the mark. The bullet mark, where Jason's genius, and his spirit, were blown through a small black hole into nothingness . . .

The telephone!

The sound nearly made me jump out of my chair. So it's mended. Oh, thank God, and they will come to take Jason away – even if the snow's bad – even if they have to bring a snow-plough, at least they can be reached by telephone –

6.00 p.m.

I'm glad I took the cassette recorder down with me. From all the jumble, something will surely emerge.

First, when the calls had been made to police etc., I rang Richard. The hall was very dark, and a faint glow from the candlelight in the sitting-room was all I had to see by (I had left my own candle upstairs). It seemed odd, standing with the latest Sony recorder hanging from a strap round my side, and dialling a nine-digit number, when there were only candles to see by, and a snow outside that could have lain there since the Bronze Age.

Richard didn't believe me for a time. I couldn't shout, because the sitting-room is too near the phone, and I must have sounded oddly remote and dispassionate, with a murdered man lying just overhead.

'Where are the police?' He sounded wary, as if my encounter with the institute for creative writing had given me a melodramatic imagination.

'They're on the way. But you must realize, Richard, the phone's been out of order until just now. Or I would have called you –'

'Hmm. Out of order last night too, was it?'

No. No, of course it wasn't and he knew it. I felt as if I'd been caught out with Jason. And I missed Jason keenly at that moment – my ally against the suspicious Richard. But such flirtatious and amorous thoughts are hardly fitting towards a corpse. I told Richard I was coming back tomorrow. As soon as they dug us out of the snow. He said it would be nice to see me. He rang off . . . And I forgot to ask him to pass on the information to John Carpenter. He probably will, though: Richard's efficient that way.

Dug us out of the snow . . .

The two burial mounds. If Muriel had in fact murdered her sister and then killed herself, the sisters placed in two mounds . . . Muriel dug up and taken to Ludlow churchyard, once the adulation and the tourists started up . . . Katerina still in the mound near the lodge, where Mrs Rees's aunt had been searching . . . hoping to dig her up. What for, why trying to dig her up . . . why should she care . . .

From the cassette, but little use it seems: We are all in the sitting-room. My call to Richard is finished. Everyone is sitting down, with the exception of Jane, who is standing under the portrait of Muriel.

When I came in from the hall, it seemed that a sudden silence fell. Am I being paranoid? Can they think *I* – no, it

119

wouldn't be possible. But do they know Jason was with me last night – yes, I think they do. Pamela Wright was audible in her room, after all – perhaps we woke her. And now she gave me a funny look – or again, am I inventing it? Would she have told Jane Cole? Yes, I'm sure she has. Jane glared at me with real hostility. Or is she simply in a state of such grief that she can show only resentment and hate?

My flurried questions didn't go down too well. Lana, Ken and Joe Merton were at the far end of the room, and the 'grown-ups', Jane and Pamela and Gertrud and Paul, were training these looks I can't be inventing on to me and every aspect of me – as a human being, as a sexual partner for Jason, as a potential murderer. They didn't seem to notice the cassette player strung over my shoulder; at least, they made no reference to it.

CATHERINE: I'm . . . I'm sorry to ask. But was . . . Jason
. . . shot? I mean, I can't see how . . .

JANE: No. There was a syringe found by the bed, wasn't
there?

CATHERINE: Oh. I see. I mean . . . could someone have
come in and . . . injected him?

JANE: They could and they did.

PAUL: Wait a minute, Jane. Until the doctor comes we
can't be sure of anything. There's no visible mark on
the body. At least, we don't properly know . . .

JANE: The doctor will find it. Do you honestly think,
Paul, that I'm going to examine my cousin's body . . .
just after . . . just after . . . Oh God.

GERTRUD: Jane. Now don't get so upset. Of course you're
not, no one expects you to. I think, Miss Catherine
Treger, that your eager journalistic questioning could
have been left to a more suitable time.

CATHERINE: Yes, yes, I'm so sorry . . .

GERTRUD: Although if anyone should know about possible marks on the body, it might be you.

So they did know. Pamela Wright was looking away from me as Gertrud said this. But I can't blame her for telling people. After all, as far as she's concerned, in the next room to her is a woman who said she'd come down on an assignment for a national newspaper, but who is in fact a killer – a jilted girlfriend, or a demented feminist.

Nevertheless, the knowledge and betrayal of another person's sexual relations is a strange thing. Pamela Wright looked distinctly uncomfortable as I gave her what couldn't help being an accusing stare. It was all the more ironic, somehow, that Jason's wife's portrait was behind her, and his cousin at her side. As if she were determined to belong in that camp – I know this is fanciful – and would give me away without batting an eyelid.

Give me away. What am I saying? They made me feel guilty downstairs, as if I had actually killed Jason, rather than slept with him. Perhaps the link between the two is stronger, still, than contemporary society will allow.

This is hardly the time for a *New Statesman and Society* piece on the *mores* of our age. Here I am, writing by the light of one candle. I am afraid. I have to admit that. Anything written is a step towards its exorcism. The candle makes huge shadows on the walls of Muriel's? – Katerina's? – room. I can feel them there, out over the expanse of snow. Hands on the window. Why did I come up here – but there are only my enemies down in the room with the piano and the tragic, beautiful portrait of Muriel. Hands. The dead sisters. Who both loved Jason so much. And Jason, lying next door, stiff and cold to their last farewells . . .

Frightened. If only I could have saved him. But I

slept so heavily. Right through the thunder, crashing like drums all round me –

A noise. At the window. No – not the hands – the rain. Or sleet, white as hands dashing against the window – at last – the end of the snow?

But another noise. Someone turning the handle – not of the door to the passage but the door into Jason's room – oh my God, who could be in there now . . .

. .

· TUESDAY ·

9.30 a.m.

I'm lucky to be alive.

I know that. My head aches abominably but I must be grateful to be alive.

Whoever it was – and I wish I could identify the tread, male or female? – came up behind me so fast that the only thing I remember is the blank page as I came down on it. Crack a joke: what a way to go at an institute for creative writing – on a blank page. No, the joke hasn't made me feel any better.

Particularly as blank pages are all that's left to me now. My notes, my diary have gone. Whoever it was took them.

Now what do I do? Do they think I'm dead?

I want a cup of tea more than anything in the world. And I must – I *must* find Richard and get out of here.

10.45 a.m.

Those white hands I wrote about so fancifully last night did turn out to be sleet which turned to rain and washed the snow away. I feel better – summoned up the courage to go downstairs and make a cup of tea in the kitchen. Or rather, Mrs Rees was there and made it for me. She was shocked by the great purple lump on my forehead – I said I'd walked into a door when the electricity wasn't on. But it's obvious from my rumpled look that I spent the night unconscious on the floor. With any luck, Mrs Rees thinks I'm a secret drinker. On no account must whoever has my notes, and wants to end my life, think I'm telling people about the attack.

Richard was out when I finally got through – had to leave an 'urgent he comes' message with Melanie!

I asked Mrs Rees about her aunt. I feel – I must – go and see her again. Solve the burial mound question. And these poor pieces of paper, which are all I have for my notes now: I'll keep them, as I did before, on my person.

The police will be here soon. The roads are hell, I suppose, with the melting snow, and the mud.

They're bound to ask me why I heard nothing, when a struggle had clearly taken place behind the wall literally a few feet away from me. I'll say I only remember the thunder . . . I wonder why, for that matter, there was no thunder last night, when the skies opened and the snow-clouds were chased away – and there *was* on the nights of freeze and snow. And what thunder . . .

I've understood something.

Drums. Drums, thunder.

I must go – tell Jane Cole – her life is in danger –

2.00 p.m.

What a terrible thing.

As I write this, Cressley crawls with police. They arrived – it was incredible – at just the moment –

In my effort to find Jane Cole I ran all over the house, and on my way I bumped into everyone who might have wanted Jason out of the way – and then me, afterwards, when they knew I was beginning to think there was something funny in the twenty-one-years-buried story of Katerina, the sister who never reappeared.

I can write with a measure of calm, because – pray God, in half an hour – Richard will arrive in his car and I shall be taken away from all this horror.

Jane wasn't in her room, which I burst into after knocking furiously. I saw – but I was too busy running to stop – that a pile of swords had been taken down from the wall and lay on the chest. A vision of Jane Cole, parrying with Byron's sword. But it wasn't funny. There was a killer who was making straight for her . . . the next target in line.

From Jane's room, I was in the musty, bad side of the house before I knew what I was doing. The dormitory door was open.

Ken was lying on his bed. He had a blissful smile on his face. Someone must have indulged him. Perhaps, in a fraught situation like this one, it was the sensible thing to do. Joe Merton was sitting near him. He looked up and moaned – yes, moaned when he saw me. He needed my help. No doubt, talk of his murderous poem was rife in the house and the police would be likely to take him first. But I didn't have time for any of that. I ran on.

Jane wasn't in the sitting-room either. Paul and Gertrud were there, and they seemed to be comforting Lana, who was a white ball pressed into the corner of the sofa. Sobs shook the sofa and Gertrud patted the ball, as if it were a frightened animal –

I ran to the barn . . . I know now how foolhardy I was,

to go alone, and without telling anyone my destination. And my legs were playing tricks on me – giving way so that I fell into the barn head first. My eyes ached – since the bump on my head I've practically had double vision – and everything seemed dark and grainy. But I had to go alone. If I'd told Paul and Gertrud what I suspected – what I felt I almost knew – they wouldn't have believed me. We'd have lost time, arguing in the sitting-room under the portrait of Muriel, while Jane died . . .

In Lana's room – or rather, the room with the Greek scenes, the sea and the hills of the sisters' youth all over the walls, Jane and Pamela Wright were standing face to face. The difference between them was that Jane's face was as pale as death and she looked suddenly shorter – while the retired housewife Pamela Wright was tall, alive suddenly, like someone who hears their name called out by a lover after a long time. Jane may have tried to pull a sword from her bedroom as Pamela Wright came to drag her away, but there was no sign of any weapon of defence. And she looked as if she were literally rooted to the spot.

Pamela's voice! That's what threw me at first. And her grey hair, loose now, and flashing black eyes –

'If you dare,' Jane Cole said.

'I dare. You. You and Jason. You took all I had. Now you give me nothing. *My* work. *My* right.'

That voice. Why didn't I think before? It wasn't a German accent, like Gertrud's: how unobservant I've been! I think of the voice behind the closed door of Jane Cole's locked room – 'I'll show her the proof!' And I think of how, in my stupidity, I immediately jumped to the conclusion that Gertrud was talking to Jane about 'The Revellers', when – yes, it was another woman speaking, saying she would show *me* the proof that she had killed

126

Katerina. The Medea poem that fell from the endpapers of Muriel's notebook ... And now who was here, who was speaking, in the same strong, Greek-flavoured voice–

'Muriel!' Jane Cole screamed.

I jumped forward into the room, with the combined weight of Paul and Gertrud Ritchie behind me. They must have guessed – thank God –

Muriel Cole was advancing on her husband's cousin with a knife as deadly as a miniature version of Lord Byron's sharpest sword. Jane's face was bright with terror ... the immobility of the Aztec features had gone ... and white spots stood out on her cheeks. The woman who was coming towards her – whom she had seen go into oblivion – who had risen from the dead to claim not her patrimony but her own estate, earned by her talent and her suffering, and her death – Pamela, Muriel –

Paul flung himself the length of the room and he and Jane fell together, Jane shrieking as she was pulled off her feet. In fury – in dismay – with all her intent in the weapon in her outstretched hand – Muriel faltered and came to a stop.

She looked up suddenly. She saw me – and Gertrud – as we walked slowly up to her – I'll never forget that walk as long as I live. In the room, painted like a cheap Greek taverna, we were entering into the power of a primal, mythical being – a Clytemnestra, maddened with grief and rage.

She stood looking at us as we came nearer. She raised the knife and held it aloft, like the sword of justice. With her hair down, she was twenty years younger. And her rage had smoothed the lines from her face and brought fire to her eyes and she was Muriel again – not poor, ill, unhappy Muriel – but triumphant Muriel, who had killed the man who had betrayed her with her sister and now would kill his accomplice, lovingly.

'Muriel!'

This time it was Gertrud who spoke. 'Muriel, give that to me.'

Muriel laughed.

The police came through the Grange and out into the yard, their boots ringing on the cobbles so that suddenly we were all transported back 500 years, to the raids on the monastery, and the hiding monks, and the smell of hay in the barn. Then the laughter – rich, olive-dark laughter – mad laughter –

The knife fell to the floor.

Muriel's laughter went on when they put her in the sitting-room, a pair of constables to guard her while the house was searched from top to bottom, while Jason's body was examined.

Will they come and question me now? I have been told to stay here, unless otherwise instructed.

Is Muriel insane? And what happened to her in those long, lonely years of her exile?

4.00 p.m.

The police inspector came. He led me down to the sitting-room. First he handed me my diary and notes, which they had found in Mrs Pamela Wright's room. 'You can be of help to us in this, Miss Treger,' he said.

But I still feel very confused. It only slowly pieces together – and that's when I remember words – single words – from the last days, and from this afternoon, when we were all under the gaze of the police inspector. The atmosphere was like mass hypnosis. The words have a powerful charge, begin to build a picture . . .

Jane: still pale, haggard. On the sofa opposite the fireplace. She stares at the woman who tried to kill her – who is in a straight-backed chair to the left of the fire – and when she is asked questions she nods and shakes her head. She is like a zombie –

Zombie The first word. What did they do to Muriel, to persuade her she must keep away from them? Why did they look uneasy when George Pendy said, 'Oh, a zombie is cheap labour, look at it that way. They do it still . . . Caribbean . . . inject a man . . . has to be buried, in the tropics, within three hours . . . certificate of death from a doctor . . . burial . . . dig him up again and he will do your bidding for the rest of his life . . .'

And Muriel did. I see it now. The Coles decided to save her – from the accusation that she was her sister's murderer, from a ruined life. They said she was dead, when in reality it was her sister who died . . . and Muriel became a zombie, a woman without a memory, who knew only to keep away from Cressley Grange and the Coles. They sent her a tiny percentage of her earnings – and in return she sent them poems! 'Newly discovered' fragments, a growing canon of work which brought a fine fortune to the Coles.

But Muriel came to life too soon. And why? Because she read words from her real past, before she became Pamela Wright, before she became one of the walking dead – in an extract from the newly discovered novel she read her words and she knew herself and she came to life.

Another word. Paul, who is at the far end of the sitting-room, by the piano, with his arm round an ashen-faced Gertrud, says when asked by the inspector what his movements were in the early hours of the morning:

'I was woken – I think most people in the house were too – by the thunder. The windows in our part of the barn don't fit very well so I got up and went to close them . . .'

Fit For all the routine questioning by the police, they must know that the woman registered here as Pamela Wright is the murderer of the dead poet upstairs, Jason Cole. The syringe Jane had taken from the floor by Jason's bed must be in their possession by now, and Pamela-Muriel's fingerprints must be on it. I shudder at the thought of the poison, and the number of syringes, Muriel has presumably brought down with her, along with her 'front', a junkie who needed to be kept in constant supply – and enough to kill the Coles too. She wrote Ken's 'promising' poems for him, I suppose – Christ!

But I must have been right to hear the word *fit* and to follow it to last night's horrible events. Because it came out, in the sitting-room and with the utmost casualness on the part of the police officers – as if they didn't care whether it was murder or not, as if it were the simplest thing in the world to say:

'There is no injection mark on Mr Cole's body, Miss Cole.'

Jane just gaped at them. We all did. Ken jumped to his feet, in that restless way he has, as if some part of him had expected arrest and trial, and he began to roam the room until he was told to sit down again. Joe Merton let out a loud groan. Even Lana, from her apparently catatonic trance, head in Gertrud's lap at the far end of the room, looked up like a startled white bird.

So . . . Muriel – Pamela went to Jason's room after hearing him leave me.

What must she have felt? Hearing us . . .

It doesn't bear thinking about.

Muriel went into his room, entering from the passage. She had given him time to fall asleep. She went to the drums, and started to play.

Thunder. The beat of the drums Muriel and Jason had once played together, building rhythms for their poetry and invoking forces better left alone.

Only Muriel knew the rhythm, the powerful beat that can induce madness and death. Hadn't they learnt it together . . .

A fit. A seizure of the heart, where Jason fought and struggled and fell, finally, back on to the bed. Dead. There had been a struggle all right, but Jason had been fighting himself. Did the warring sides of his nature rise up then, to the terrible throb of the drum, and the penitent, God-fearing man go into combat to the last with the pagan god of death? . . .

♦

After the disclosure of Jason's unmarked body, we all sat in silence for a time. Paul and Gertrud were studiously not looking at each other: I could see they didn't believe in death from natural causes for one minute. Are we supposed to believe Jason had a heart attack? On the anniversary of his wife's death, when the wife herself turns up in person to confront him?

But of course the police don't know about Muriel yet.

Jane had her head in her hands. She'll have to tell them. How far will she go? Tell them there was a sister, who died – no, how can she do that? Where's the body, then, Miss Cole?

131

And now *I* have to confront something.

Suppose – if – no one guesses the drums, Muriel's particular, vicious method of dispatching her faithless husband into the next world – do I tell them? Or do I keep secret the grisly details of this most horrifying story? For this is what I believe must have happened – twenty-one years ago.

♦

Muriel's sister Katerina comes from Greece to stay at Cressley Grange.

Katerina and Jason fall in love and have an affair. Muriel goes out and tries to kill herself in a motor accident, but fails. She becomes heavily reliant on morphine.

Muriel's jealousy and misery grow acute. One night – one night with a new moon, and snow like these last days here, Muriel leaves the barn, where she has banished herself, in pure masochism, so that Katerina can take her room, take her place for Jason as he writes 'The Revellers'.

Muriel goes up the stairs, along the passage –

She comes in here. She carries her syringe, which is always with her in these days of unbearable pain.

She injects Katerina and drags her out to the barn. She goes back to her old room, gets into bed, waits for Jason's nightly, adulterous visit to his sister-in-law.

Whether he came through that communicating door or not, we'll never know. But in the morning, in the barn, Katerina is found dead. (Who found her? I feel sure, suddenly, it was Mr and Mrs Rees. They're in on this, somehow.) Katerina must have regained consciousness for a moment, because she managed to scratch the initials M U on the floor by the bed. What was she trying to tell? That it was Muriel who had killed her – that it was murder? Because the inevitable suicide badge is carefully by the bed, too: the empty syringe – with which she scratched the letters – a syringe like the one Muriel has kept for this night of retribution.

♦

Do I really believe this is what happened? That Muriel, the victim of male oppression, the precursor of the great wave of feminism which has spread over the Western world since her death – that this heroine, this suffering woman, was in fact a murderer? And more, a murderer in cold blood?

If Katerina . . . unhappy too, at the impossible situation between the three of them, had committed suicide that night . . .? Isn't it more likely?

But in that case, why did Muriel have to disappear? The Coles must have known what happened: they knew Katerina's death couldn't be passed off as a suicide. Because there was a witness. Muriel had been seen – didn't Mrs Rees say something, to the effect that her aunt used to sleep in at the Grange, and only after the death of Muriel Cole did she and her husband move to the lodge?

Yes, she – or all three of them – must have seen Muriel, dragging the body of her dying sister down those infernal stairs and out through the sitting-room French windows to the cobbled yard and the barn . . .

5.30 p.m.

No sign of Richard. The police are still downstairs, but what will happen when they go? They'll take Jason's body

133

with them, but will they leave us all here? Or will Mr Rees turn up, imperturbable, the perfect chauffeur, and drive all the 'students' to Hereford station? The end of another course in creative writing. A crash course in death.

Muriel will kill me, if we are forced to stay on here tonight. Like she tried to before, when she knew I had found her Medea poem . . . the notebook she deliberately placed amongst the most provocative books, so I was bound to see it – with the quotes on suicide just to stress that Muriel Cole really did end her life twenty-one years ago . . . a pity for her those other, forgotten, murderous lines fell into my hands . . . yes, I really had to go then . . . just as I was puzzling out the extraordinary, unbelievable story of her life. When she came snooping into my room, and read this diary – and saw I was beginning to know – and casually, too, falling into bed with her husband.

Don't let her get away with it. Muriel murdered her sister. She returned to murder her husband, and then his cousin. The police saw her, in the luridly painted room in the barn with Jane Cole.

Arrest her. Put her away.

6.00 p.m.

There's only one thing to do. I have to assume Richard didn't get the message, or Melanie didn't give it to him, out of spite. I have to get out of here. I go down and tell the police I need to be taken to Hereford police station, where I would like to make a statement regarding the death of Jason Cole. It's too dangerous – my God, my

134

hands are shaking. What fear I have now of that evil woman.

I'll tell them. Muriel Cole killed her sister, I'll say, and the Coles turned that into the suicide of Muriel Cole. Very ingenious. Oh, very.

Clever, competent Muriel. Who had the presence of mind, when she woke from her long trance, to find a juvenile heroin addict and pronounce him a genius and carry him with her to Cressley Grange. Her mind was always made up, that she would kill Jason, if she had to, with the secret, killing beat of the drums, the beat they learned together. But if she failed – if Jason was too strong for her, then she had 'Ken's syringe' – and she would use it too, as Jason struggled to get out of his sleep and the terrible beat of the drums. Ken, the murderer. Muriel Cole would not stop at anything by now.

Of course. What a fool I've been. I must run, if I want to catch the Reeses . . .

Of course, the police must suspect that Jason was poisoned. They'll hold suspects until after the autopsy. They must be interviewing them, one by one now – and even if Richard does come, they won't let me go with him.

I am in danger from all of them. It will all come out – and Muriel will tell them Jason was with me – and Richard will know. And I will be chief suspect –

Must find them. Tell the police. In the churchyard at Ludlow, in Muriel's grave, they'll find an empty coffin. In the artificial hill, at the lodge end of the drive, they'll find Katerina.

So easy for them all to say I was the last person to be with Jason, that I poisoned him. (But try and be calm; they haven't had the autopsy yet; they will find nothing. I am *right* about the drums.) They'll say I must have been an old girlfriend of his – come to try to marry him, killing him in the end, when he turned me down. Why should the police believe me when I say Jason was a stranger to me when I came here on Friday?

No, I can't go down into the hall by the sitting-room and risk being held back by them. I'll have to go the other way. Through the communicating door into Jason's room. Down the steps into the Martyr's Room. Out of the Martyr's Room and down the spiral stairs into the long refectory. Then – into the main hall – out the front door – luckily, it's raining, and no sign of the moon. It should take me no more than three minutes to run to the lodge.

I don't want to go into Jason's room . . .

9.00 p.m.

Now I am safe, if only for a few hours, I can admit to my guilt.

For I was wrong. I accused Muriel Cole of the murder of her sister. I did just what they wanted me to do . . .

And if it hadn't been for Gertrud, poor Gertrud whom I despised and laughed at when she tried to show me the truth . . .

And Mrs Rees's aunt . . .

◆

But I will try to explain. As I ran through Jason's room in my headlong rush for freedom – and without glancing at that white sheeted form on the bed, face covered below the leers and scowls of the masks – Gertrud ran in from the far door and held her arms wide so that I had no choice but to stop.

'Catherine!' she said. And she handed me the paper – I could see the words 'For Katerina' typed at the top of the sheet – while with her other hand she waved violently at me as if forbidding me at all costs to read it.

'Don't you see?' Gertrud said. 'There was never such a person as Katerina. Jason made her up. When he tired of Muriel – and when she maddened him, as she did so many times – he invented a sister for her, an ideal double if you like. In his poem and his fantasy he lived with her. And I, Catherine, I am sorry. I was so jealous of you that I told you Katerina really existed.'

'Ulalume,' I said, as if some schoolgirl memory of Poe and my school in the village in Canada had suddenly come back to me.

'Yes, yes. I know that Muriel had no sister. But you see it was very useful . . . for Jane Cole . . .'

Of course, I thought, as Gertrud Ritchie stood there, still using the fragment of 'The Revellers' like a truce flag in the war between us over the love of Jason. Of course it was useful for Jane Cole. She used her cousin's fantasy to persuade Muriel that she had a real rival, that she had a 'sister' who had supplanted her in Jason's affections. She told her she must murder the sister . . . and Muriel even wrote some lines – the ones tucked in the back of her diary – to show the kind of vehement hatred expected of her in the circumstances.

But, obviously, she didn't murder Katerina at all. There was no one there, even if she had had it in her to kill another woman; but Jane Cole, as Muriel's morphine addiction deepened, even persuaded her to move from her room to the barn, to make it 'easier' for Jason to write his epic poem.

137

In the barn, twenty-one years ago, Jane came and – unaware that the nurse who had just left had already given sedation – saw Muriel Cole administer to herself a large dose of morphine and heroin. All there was time for was for Muriel to scratch M U on the tiles by the narrow bed where she had been confined ever since this mythical 'sister' had taken Jason away from her.

Whether he knew that his cousin Jane Cole was playing this devilish part is impossible to say. Great poets are absent-minded – they can be if they're male, I suppose, and don't have to attend to the trivia of daily life.

Perhaps Jason turned a blind eye to his cousin's game. Certainly he can't have stopped her from showing Muriel a few lines of the poem he had addressed to 'Katerina', the ideal of Muriel as she should have been. And, not surprisingly, they drove her further into drugs and despair.

For Katerina
> She strides the air
>   on a swan, on a bull.
> She becomes one
> with the heavenly twins.
>   She sees her sister, her sister
>   In the four-gated city where she sleeps
> As I lie with her
> In a snow of uncertainty
> A sea stupor
>   You did it
>   You didn't drown this time
>   You lay under the heads of poppies
>   By the sun-dark sea
> In Missolonghi.

Gertrud, who had allowed me only a few seconds to read

138

the lines, now removed them for the last time and allowed herself a grim smile.

'There's no doubt about it,' she said. 'Jason did know. The syringe he saw as one of Byron's swords – he often used to allude to Jane's collection in that way. He knew that Jane saw his wife induce her coma. Now, what are you going to write about that?'

'But the old lady at the lodge,' I said, 'she seemed to think I was Katerina. So . . . surely . . . there's a possibility there had been a Katerina at some time?'

'The old lady was here at the time of Muriel's illness,' Gertrud said. 'And it was put about that a Greek sister, very beautiful but very reclusive, was staying at the Grange. No wonder she thought, in a state of near-senile confusion, that it must have been you.'

'Thank you,' I said. Even the sound of steps on the stairs couldn't stop me feeling vain and pleased at the compliment – and all relating to a woman who hadn't even existed!

Yet it was of the line by Emily Dickinson that I thought as I slipped away down the secret staircase into the Martyr's Room and then down the spiral into a hall emptied by the hunters as they swarmed up the main staircase in search of their prey.

'The chill' – as I ran out into the snow through a side door I had found that night when I helped Lana to her lurid dreams; 'the stupor' – as poor Muriel's trance froze her to herself and to her poetry; 'the letting go' – as I ran, unafraid of the cold or the coming dark, through woodland to the open road.

✦ EPILOGUE ✦

STATEMENT FROM MS MELANIE BARRATT
Sydney, Australia, 9 January 1989.

Subsequent to the nervous breakdown and hospitalization of my brother Richard's former room-mate Catherine Treger, I the undersigned would like the following points to be made absolutely clear.

The discovery of Ms Treger's diaries in a wood in Herefordshire – and the irresponsible publication of them – has caused considerable distress and annoyance to our family.

Distasteful though the subject may be, we are obliged to restate the facts of the case, obvious though they may seem to any person not suffering, as poor Catherine Treger was, from confusion and near-dementia, culminating in a full-scale psychotic condition.

1. Jason Cole died of natural causes, which can be ascertained by anyone wishing to do so by obtaining a copy of the death certificate.
2. Muriel Cole, as is extremely well known, died of a self-administered morphine overdose in 1967 and is buried in Ludlow churchyard.
3. Pamela Wright is a bona fide part-time teacher of English at Turlington Green School, Birmingham. She has

been well known in the neighbourhood for over forty years and keeps in close contact with her family.

We therefore request that media attention be withdrawn from us at the soonest possible opportunity, and that a fantasy – the work of a disturbed brain – should be recognized as being just that.

Melanie Barratt

Telephone interview with Jane Cole, 9 January, at Cressley Grange, for the *Clarion* newspaper.

CLARION: But can you tell me, Miss Cole, where you think Catherine got all this information from?

JANE *glacial*: What information?

CLARION: Well ... er ... the return of Muriel Cole ... and the sister who died ... was murdered ...

JANE: Excuse me, young woman. Have you ever heard of the Castalian spring?

CLARION: No ... I'm afraid ...

JANE: It is our only stimulant here. Its waters bring poetic inspiration, which should be enough for most mortals. But I am sorry to inform you that Catherine Treger imported spirits – which, I may say, is strictly forbidden – to Cressley Grange. After drinking heavily one night, she became unconscious and appeared with a large bump on her head, pretending to Mrs Rees, our ex-housekeeper here, that she had walked into a door, or some such nonsense.

CLARION: If you don't mind my saying so, Miss Cole, that doesn't sound too bad a crime.

JANE: Indeed, there is no crime. Catherine hallucinated – and wrote down her fantasies – a most unattractive and unpleasant way of thanking us for our hospitality here, I must say.

141

CLARION: But . . . isn't that what people on the Cressley course are expected to do, Miss Cole?
Silence. The receiver has been replaced.

From the *Ludlow Advertiser*, 11 January 1989

Flossie, a King Charles spaniel, taking a stroll with its mistress in the grounds of Cressley Grange, home of the late Jason Cole, came home with an unusual kind of bone, police reports said yesterday in Cardiff, where the bone has been taken for forensic examination.

Dug out of a low mound near the lodge (now empty) by Flossie, the bone was immediately confiscated by her owner, Mrs Millicent Pratt, 52, and taken to Ludlow police station.

No comment is yet available on the age of the relic, though both Iron and Bronze Age burial sites are known to exist in the woods at Cressley.